The Garden
and the Jungle

The Garden and the Jungle

HOW THE WEST SEES
THE WORLD

EDWY PLENEL

Translated from the French by Luke Leafgren

OTHER PRESS
New York

Epigraph by Édouard Glissant and Patrick Chamoiseau, "When the Walls Fall: National Identity Beyond the Law" (2007), in *Manifestos*, ed. Édouard Glissant and Patrick Chamoiseau, trans. Betsy Wing and Matt Reeck (London: Goldsmiths Press, 2022), 29.

Production editor: Yvonne E. Cárdenas
Text designer: Patrice Sheridan
This book was set in Garamond Premier Pro by
Alpha Design & Composition of Pittsfield, NH

10 9 8 7 6 5 4 3 2 1

Library of Congress Cataloging-in-Publication Data
Names: Plenel, Edwy author | Leafgren, Luke translator
Title: The garden and the jungle : how the west sees the world / Edwy Plenel ; translated from the French by Luke Leafgren.
Other titles: Jardin et la jungle. English | Address to Europe on how it sees the world
Description: New York : Other Press, [2025] | Original title "Le jardin et la jungle: Adresse a l'Europe sur l'idee quelle se fait du monde" published by Editions La Decouverte in 2024. | Includes bibliographical references.
Identifiers: LCCN 2025004460 (print) | LCCN 2025004461 (ebook) | ISBN 9781635425598 paperback | ISBN 9781635425604 ebook
Subjects: LCSH: European Union countries—Politics and government | European Union countries—Foreign relations | Exceptionalism—Europe | Equality—Political aspects
Classification: LCC JN30 .P59913 2025 (print) | LCC JN30 (ebook) | DDC 320.94—dc23/eng/20250520
LC record available at https://lccn.loc.gov/2025004460
LC ebook record available at https://lccn.loc.gov/2025004461

The time will come when the desire to dominate, to impose laws, to establish empires, when the pride at being the strongest and when the arrogance of controlling the truth will be considered the surest signs of barbarity at work in the history of humanity.

—ÉDOUARD GLISSANT AND PATRICK CHAMOISEAU,
"WHEN THE WALLS FALL: NATIONAL IDENTITY
BEYOND THE LAW" (2007)

CONTENTS

INTRODUCTION TO THE AMERICAN EDITION

THE GARDEN AND THE JUNGLE was published in France in September 2024. This address to Europe on how it sees the world reaches beyond the European continent to the entire West, of which the United States of America is the dominant power. It was written in the shadow of two ongoing wars, that of Russia against Ukraine and that of Israel against Gaza, and in the ever-present memory of the catastrophes for which Europe is responsible, from colonialism to Nazism. Its goal was to question those imperial claims to superiority, domination, and power which have not ceased injecting barbarity into the heart of civilization.

Two months later, the election of Donald Trump to a second term as president of the United States served to justify this alarm. Ever since January 20, 2025, the empire has been striking back, and it's an empire of radical political evil: the assertive denial of any shared humanity, the universal rejection of equal rights, the international affirmation of the law of the strongest, the proclamation of power without limits or principles. The second presidency of Donald Trump carries North American imperialism to its apogee by adopting, without doublespeak or false pretenses, the all-encompassing goals of conquest and domination, of greed and self-interest, contained within the claim to the greatness—economic, military, cultural—of the United States of America with respect to the rest of the world.

The reference to the cinematic saga *Star Wars* (that interstellar battle in which *The Empire Strikes Back* is the fifth episode) is fitting, given that science fiction is the mental universe of the new feudalism that, under Trump, has conquered the levers of power in Washington: a technophilic oligarchy launched by the digital revolution to a stratospheric degree of wealth that grants unwavering confidence in the impunity of its power. Just like its most emblematic representative, Elon Musk, who purchased his place as unelected co-president, it stands explicitly with the dark side of the Force.

Its guiding principle is limitlessness: nothing can hinder its desire on any register: power, wealth, conquest, control, extractivism, and so on. The greatness it claims is a catastrophe foretold. Make America

Great Again, the MAGA that the campaign took as its single slogan, means that nothing must oppose the will to power of the United States of America. Not only the planet Mars, but also sovereign nations—Canada, Panama, or Denmark by way of Greenland. Not only undesirable humans, those migrants whose deportation is being organized, but also foreign goods, in a return to the most antiquated trade wars. To say nothing of democracy itself, already thrown by the wayside and reduced to the simple legitimacy conferred by elections, abandoning all other checks and balances.

Trump's presidency is not the new avatar of some social conservatism. It embodies a savagery emerging within the heart of civilization, just as happened in Europe, when fascism and Nazism put the fate of all of humanity at risk. This flat-out counterrevolution takes precise aim at the jolt that occurred the day after the Second World War. The moment when awareness of the catastrophes and ravages of unbridled power—as testified by the millions of victims of genocide and other crimes against humanity, which would henceforth receive legal definitions—led to the proclamation of universal human rights and the invention of the diplomatic rules of the United Nations.

Trump says it and does it: he wants a clean break from precisely this heritage. Against the promise of equal rights that has not stopped inspiring battles for emancipation, he positions the law of superiority, which takes identity as its pretext, anchored in the soil and the blood, in blind chance of birth and lines of descent. No more common humanity, no more international community, no more solidarity and fraternity: what's right is only what I judge to be good for my people, my nation, my power. Nothing else. Such a political program is fundamentally separatist: it breaks with the ideal of a shared world, where human beings, just like the nature of which they are part, are in relationship, ineluctably interconnected, intermixed, and interdependent.

Apartheid is its watchword. It was in 1948, the same year of the Universal Declaration of Human Rights, that the Afrikaner regime of South Africa enacted its laws of separation. The establishment of this racial separation makes a distinction in all aspects of daily life—housing, work, movement, marriage, and so on—between the white population, decreed to be superior, and other categories—Blacks, Indians, mixed race. It echoes the paradigm of the world that gave birth to the European disaster: the hierarchy of humanities that gives rise to the colonial and imperial lunacies of conquest and grandeur, and which inevitably proceeds to deny, pursue, repulse, or exterminate the Other, erasing them in every instance.

The presidency of Donald Trump proclaims itself to be an apartheid empire, adopting its ideology and project. This monstrosity is making its comeback on a global scale. It is the program of far-right groups in all their various forms, which, by asserting migration to be an existential threat, attack equal rights for all. This infernal program inevitably sets its sights on all diversity of affected peoples, targeting racialized and discriminated individuals, women's rights, gender issues, LGBTQI+ struggles, and more broadly, all supposed minorities, whose assertiveness threatens the conservatives who claim to hold the majority.

This is the source of Elon Musk's double Nazi salute on the day of Donald Trump's inauguration, preceded by many other provocations that testify to his racism, anti-Semitism, and fascism. Like Peter Thiel and David Sacks, two other figures of the oligarchic techno-feudalism that has assumed power in the United States, Elon Musk comes from that South Africa of separation and segregation, of the rejection of humanity and the sorting of human beings, in short, of the radical rejection of equal rights.

This symbol encapsulates the moment of truth we are facing, the certainty that the worst is upon us: an old world of predation, which clings to privileges that entail unbearable injustices for many, gives birth to monsters with the aim of eradicating, once and for all, the hope for a better world: less unjust, less violent, less destructive. And so, we are confronted by a civilizational challenge, one that eclipses every secondary feud and fleeting dispute.

I wrote this book in the hope that people will finally see what is happening. And I make a wish that, in the face of this danger, its publication in the United States will accompany a renewed commitment by the American people to the democratic ideals upon which their nation was founded.

February 24, 2025
Paris

ADDRESS TO EUROPE

EUROPE, WHAT HAVE YOU made of your promise? The promise of a shared humanity and a universal law?

You profess it, and at the same time, you persist in undermining it. Ever since you proclaimed it, you've never ceased contradicting it. Yesterday, you extolled it in your own house, even while you vandalized it elsewhere. Today, more than ever, you brandish it whenever it serves to protect you from an aggressor, but then you renounce it when the West, that political reality born from your projection upon the world, becomes in turn the aggressor, and it attacks, invades, occupies, destroys, exterminates.

It is certainly a long and old history, a history of hypocrisy and supremacy, of predation and justification, of self-love and fear of the Other. But enough with false pretenses! From now on, the whole world knows it and sees it clearly. And moving forward, it is all too easy for the various ruling powers, unjust though they may be, to turn that fraud to their own advantage. No people is fooled, not even your own, who more and more are surrendering to the siren calls of identity and of force, of rejecting equal rights and abandoning an interconnected world.

And this is how, Europe, that you race to your own demise, having ruined that which made your power true. Not the provisional and ephemeral power of wealth, both money and possessions, but the lasting and vital power of ideas, utopian dreams, and emancipations.

1 ▸ THE BRUGES SPEECH

HERE ARE THE WORDS, uttered between two wars, of a disoriented West, of a Europe that has lost its way.

Smug words, superior and proud, entirely self-satisfied. Words that are the source of persistent misunderstanding with the rest of the world, its peoples, and its hopes, and that prop up this continent of ours, together with its North American ally. Sentences that show, like a photographic negative, everything that we must urgently champion, if we wish to escape the emerging catastrophe of a return, everywhere in the world, of the brown-shirted horsemen of the inegalitarian apocalypse, those on the far right who embrace an identitarian ideology that rejects the Other and the elsewhere, the strange and the stranger, the different and the dissimilar, the plural and the diverse.

On October 13, 2022, the European commissioner for foreign affairs gave an inaugural address at the new European Diplomatic Academy. The academy is in the Belgian city of Bruges, a city that in the seventeenth century was at the heart of Europe's mercantile conquest of the world, which was driven by the dynamics of invention and the expansion of capitalism. It was at that moment that some historians credit the city with the birth of the word *bourse*, meaning a meeting place for bankers, merchants, stockbrokers, courtiers, and others who served as financiers. In Bruges, it was at the Hôtel des Bourses—which took its name from the bourgeois Van der Beurse family—that those assemblies of exchange and commerce took place.[1]

In the wake of the conquest of the Americas, through which Europe enlarged and glorified itself by means of plunder and enslavement, our economic world went on to invent itself in laboratory cities, particularly in Venice, Florence, and Genoa. Yet it was 250 kilometers (150 miles) from Bruges, in Amsterdam, where the decisive invention took place that dominates us today, anticipating financial capitalism with its fluidity, its speed, its emptiness, its malignancy: a bourse, that is, a stock market, where the speculative game burned most bright. Propping up the prime stocks of those market speculators were the actions of the Dutch East India Company, followed by the Dutch West India Company. Companies that turned cargoes of slaves into merchandise to be auctioned off: men, women, and children, their humanity denied, carried off, purchased, traded, chained, beaten, deported, sold, violated, exhausted, subjugated, exploited, destroyed...

I recall this history so that, when reading the words below from the de facto minister of foreign affairs of the European Union, we might bear in mind this long epoch of injustice, this crime against humanity, which propelled Europe to the top of the world. So that we might remember this unredeemed legacy, which always prevents others from taking us, all Europeans, at our word. However powerful and productive they may be, the great abstract principles that we proclaim as universal were promptly ruined by self-interest and conquest, by greed and ownership.

A European novelist bore witness to the nineteenth century as observed in his life as a sailor and officer on merchant marine ships. Polish by birth but educated as French before he became English, he summed it up, without any long and tedious explanation, simply by saying "The horror! The horror!" Those are the final words, pronounced in "a cry that was no more than a breath" by Kurtz, the antihero of *Heart of Darkness*,[2] the novella by Joseph Conrad that inspired the Francis Ford Coppola film about the imperialist war waged by the United States in Vietnam, *Apocalypse Now*.

Sent to the Congo—at that time the personal property of Leopold II, king of Belgium, a criminal monarch whose predatory brutality is tallied at no less than ten million dead[3]—Kurtz is commissioned to write a report for "the International Society for the Suppression of Savage Customs." "A beautiful piece of writing," comments the narrator upon reading those seventeen pages, even while acknowledging "ominous" passages. For example, Kurtz writes that we whites "must necessarily appear to them in the nature of supernatural beings—we approach them with the might of a deity." Later, he asserts, "By the simple exercise of our will we can exert a power for good practically unbounded."

These pages give the idea of "an exotic Immensity ruled by an august Benevolence," as summarized by Conrad, in the voice of Captain Marlow, who goes up the Congo River to search for Kurtz, who has mysteriously disappeared into the African jungle. But then Marlow adds, "Unless a kind of note at the foot of the last page, scrawled evidently much later, in an unsteady hand, may be regarded as the exposition of a method." That note reads, "Exterminate all the brutes!" This is no invention of fiction: this "method" is the bloody truth of civilizing conquest. Every colonization was also an extermination.

The jungle is the other word for the darkness that pervades Conrad's novel. It is "impenetrable," "tangled," "colossal...so dark-green as to be almost black," and, above all, "the hearts of wild men"; a strange and hostile world where "that mysterious life of the wilderness" reigns. The jungle, then: strange, a stranger, menacing, dangerous.

When I sketched out this book—the writing of which was repeatedly overtaken by heart-rending realities, from the massacre of Gaza to the war in Ukraine, to say nothing of New Caledonia, that hillock bearing witness to colonialism, or the neofascist peril that has arrived in France, with the National Rally, and in the United States, with Donald Trump, both of which are sponsors and supporters of Vladimir Putin's Russia—a nocturnal exhibition was being held in the Jardin des Plantes in Paris: Illuminating the Jungle, it was called. It is as marvelous as it is menacing. In an uncanny articulation of the challenges of our inextricably interdependent world, this artificial presentation of nature, which has become an annual Parisian watering hole, is the work of a Chinese company and installed by traveling workers. On an informational placard, I read an introduction to "the jungle," a word of Sanskrit origin that "stimulates our imagination" because it "evokes distant lands, unexplored forests, a great beauty but also numerous dangers and the fear of the unknown."

Indeed, the fear of the unknown. The world changes, pivots, spins around, changes tack. And it eludes us. For better or worse—for the better, depending on what people will do with it, if, at least, they do not abandon the obvious fact of a shared salvation, that quest for bread, for peace and for justice. Above all, if they manage to break the shackles of privileges and conservatisms that prevent them from freely choosing a better fate.

It is this fear of the unknown—of an entire world, insofar as it invents itself independently of Europe, away from or outside it—that I read in this speech, delivered in Belgium at the new European Diplomatic Academy, on October 13, 2022, by Josep Borrell, then vice president of the European Commission (2019–24), high representative of the Union for Foreign Affairs and Security Policy. It was more than seven months after the start of the Russian war of conquest against Ukraine on February 24, 2022, and one year before the start of the Israeli war of vengeance against the Palestinian enclave of Gaza, as a response to the civilian massacres committed by Hamas on October 7, 2023.

Here, then, is what he said:

> Yes, Europe is a garden. We have built a garden. Everything works. It is the best combination of political freedom, economic prosperity, and social cohesion

that humankind has been able to build—these three things together... The rest of the world... is not exactly a garden... Most of the rest of the world is a jungle, and the jungle could invade the garden. The gardeners should take care of it, but they will not protect the garden by building walls. A nice small garden surrounded by high walls to prevent the jungle from coming in is not going to be a solution. Because the jungle has a strong growth capacity, and the wall will never be high enough to protect the garden. The gardeners have to go to the jungle. Europeans have to be much more engaged with the rest of the world. Otherwise, the rest of the world will invade us, by different ways and means.[4]

These remarks are all the more notable since they do not come from a neoconservative reactionary, an imperialist believer in the clash of civilizations, that self-fulfilling prophecy that embroiled the United States and its European allies in a never-ending war, for which the invasion of Iraq in 2003 was the accelerator. No, Josep Borrell is a man associated with the left, a longtime militant of the Spanish Social Workers' Party (PSOE), longtime deputy in the Spanish parliament, with stints as minister before serving as president of the European parliament, and then joining the executive branch of the European Union.

Quickly realizing the disastrous effect of his speech, even as Europe was searching for allies in the face of a resurgent Russian imperialism, both aggressive and conquering, Borrell attempted to diminish it. Defending himself against any kind of "colonial Eurocentrism," he explained his metaphor as a return of the "law of the jungle," encapsulated by Russia's invasion of Ukraine, a symbol of the "power politics" that entails an accelerated militarization and a legitimization of the primacy of force over right. Clearly a lame explanation, even as it neglects long eras of unilateral acts committed by North American power. Needing to retrench, Borrell concluded by conceding that "Yes, the Western world has also at times contributed to the misuse of force."[5] A weak line of defense that, one year later, would not only be struck, but shattered, under the obvious double standard shown by Europe and the United States toward Ukraine and Gaza, depending on whether the war is Russian or Israeli, and whether the civilian victims are European or Palestinian.

In January 2024, the European commissioner himself had to agree, underlining this contrast between a Europe unanimous in condemning the Russian aggression against Ukraine, and a Europe divided when faced with Israel's war of extermination against Gaza: "Our lack of unity has weakened our credibility when it comes to defending international law...It is difficult to appeal to the judgment of the international community and the United Nations vote in one case and not in the other. This conundrum presents significant political and moral dilemmas for Europe that must be faced with clarity and courage."[6] Coming too late as it did, this demurral was nothing but a confession of impotence with regard to Israel. For even as the extremist prime minister of that state, Benjamin Netanyahu, shamelessly violates international laws that he couldn't care less about, he has been fully supported, apart from a few ineffectual scoldings. At the same time, he has not stopped evoking the image of the garden as an outpost of civilization, confronting a jungle where barbarians prowl: "You must clearly understand, you, the West, that it is a war of civilization! Israel is on the front lines. Its victory against terrorism will be your victory."[7]

The catastrophe begins with words that habituate us to the worst.[8] The Frenchman Gustave Le Bon predicted it: "The power of words is so great that it suffices to designate in well-chosen terms the most odious things to make them acceptable to crowds."[9] The German Victor Klemperer documented it: "Words can be like tiny doses of arsenic: they are swallowed unnoticed."[10] By essentializing Europe as a superior, civilizing, and beneficent force, this opposition of two words, garden and jungle, surrenders to ideologies of inequality and administers the poison of identitarian refrains. Indeed, the speech by Josep Borrell concludes with an appeal to oppose this identitarian terrain, hoping to open the door to identities that are not closed, but that allow for relationship, for an integration of "you and me," which he defines as "the beauty of the European experience." It's an abusive compliment, considering that the metaphor of garden and jungle is a total contradiction of what he is trying to do. It separates and opposes rather than connecting and bringing near.

"Keep the garden. Be good gardeners," he concludes, by way of inviting future European diplomats to "take care of...the jungle outside." The heritage of a persistent colonial mentality, this good civilizational conscience, simultaneously paternalistic and essentialist, paves the way for opponents of equal rights, all those resolved to undermine this emancipatory promise that makes no distinction regarding origin, birth, condition, appearance, religion, gender, or race. In other words, the enemies of the human race, in the sense that they deny our common and equal humanity. A jungle threatening to invade the garden irresistibly evokes a "great replacement," that conspiracy theory and murderous ideology that unites, everywhere in the world, the far right in their desire for purity and wish to reject the Other.

Yet there is no need to go searching within the now-ascendant neofascism to measure the ravages of this language and the unconsciousness it reveals, which rejects the world and the Other. Haven't terms such as "decivilization" and "immigrationism," borrowed from the vocabulary of identitarian circles of xenophobes and racists, become official words pronounced by a head of state who was himself twice elected as a bulwark against the far right? Such words were heard in 2023 and 2024, after the Bruges speech, from the mouth of Emmanuel Macron, president of a republic. This is the same president responsible for the 2021 law against "separatism," yet another word that divides and separates, sorting good from evil, setting the good French against the bad French, team garden against team jungle.

The Jungle Grows Back: already, in 2018, that was the title of a book by the American neoconservative Robert Kagan, who called for the United States not to surrender to isolationism but to intervene on an even greater basis, militarily of course, to tame this "imperiled world."[11] Although Kagan resides in Brussels, where he associates with Europe's elites, I cannot say what amnesia has led a Spanish socialist to take up his refrain, almost word for word. According to Josep Borrell, the liberal world order is fragile and impermanent, which is the central point of

Kagan, who writes, "The liberal world order is like a garden, ever under siege from the forces of history, the jungle whose vines and weeds constantly threaten to overwhelm it." Unless, perhaps, the Bruges speech, like a Freudian slip, is the confession of a common imagination that goes beyond political labels: the same language of power, which is to say of economic interests and states dominating others.

Under the apparently good intention of critiquing the partisans of a fortress Europe, barricaded behind high walls, Borrell thus bears witness to the persistent blindness of the tenants of a powerful Europe that dictates its own law while pretending to be the custodian of the just and the good. In the voice of European diplomacy, he tells the world that Europe still does not accept that the world doesn't exist in its own image. Not only has Europe, together with its North American ally, the United States, not renounced dominion over the world, but it persists in believing itself to be the incarnation of civilization, culture, the good, and the just, confronting the barbarities of a global arena where savagery, darkness, and evil reign.

And yet it is here that Europe goes astray and loses itself, turning its back on the values of humanism, universality, and equality, which it claims for its own by virtue of proclaiming them. By persisting in contradicting and betraying those values, Europe separates itself from a diverse world that henceforth will forge its own path. As long as Europe, together with its political expression, the West, does not renounce its desire for power, it will rally against itself the resentment of all those peoples who, over five centuries, have suffered the bitter experience of their domination. For when the Bruges speech sounds the alarm about a jungle, that jungle is none other than our own, a jungle produced by the blindness of conquest and exploitation. And far from being an ideal model, our garden was the site of the worst barbarities, where, in the name of some identities being superior to others, the crime of genocide was committed.

The Zone of Interest, a film by Jonathan Glazer that won the Grand Prix at the Cannes Film Festival in 2023, carries us into a garden surrounded by high walls, topped with barbed wire to protect it from its jungle. A "nice small garden," to recall Josep Borrell's phrase, tended with meticulous care by the mistress of the place, who selects the plants and uproots the weeds. A veritable "paradise of flowers," as her husband writes in his memoirs, where "there was always something new and interesting."[12] The gardener, Hedwig Höss, is the wife of Rudolf Höss, commandant of Auschwitz, and the garden outside their house abuts the extermination camp, where, over the course of five years, in the largest concentration camp of the Third Reich, more than 1,100,000 men, women, and children, 90 percent of them Jews, were murdered.[13]

We are not the garden, and the world around us is not the jungle. Just the opposite: our European garden invented its own barbaric jungles, those of the destruction of man by man. And until they have reckoned with all the consequences, Europe and the West will continue to get it wrong. To go astray, and in the end to allow the return—or indeed, the triumph—of those criminal ideologies and destructive forces that during the last century plunged the world into night. We will ward off these dangers, so terribly menacing, only by making a break with this vision of superiority and power. By taking the measure of Europe's own responsibility for the disorders it claims to avert. And in founding anew a Europe that cares for the fragility of the world and of the living.

In other words, by promoting a radically different way of seeing, not only as democratic and social, egalitarian and humanist, but also as ecological, decolonial, feminist, anti-imperialist, hospitable, concerned for minorities and the excluded, not tolerating any discrimination, refusing to impose its law upon everyone else. Otherwise, our own jungle will find its way back, laying waste to the gardens of the world.

2 ▶ THE BATTLE FOR RIGHTS

IN 1790, ONE YEAR after the French Revolution began, Immanuel Kant invented the "art of landscape gardening." In *Critique of Judgement*, the philosopher made it one of the fine arts, drawing an equivalence between "the art of the beautiful *depicting of nature* and that of the beautiful *arrangement of its products*."[1] An intellectual recluse who cloistered himself within his own home, Kant went outside only once each day for a walk that nourished his reflections upon life, in all its diversity and infinitude.

A philosopher ahead of his times, Kant was the person who introduced geography to the university when he delivered, between 1756 and 1796, forty-nine cycles of a lecture course suffused with anthropology. In fact, after logic and metaphysics, this was the subject he taught most frequently. Inventing human geography before it was designated as such, his encyclopedic *Physical Geography* would be published in 1802 from manuscripts and notes.[2] Instead of the cosmopolitan light that this philosopher is famous for, this book reveals its shadows.

"The nations of the southern hemisphere are on the lowest level of humanity,"[3] we read. It is but one example among a thousand of prejudice and hierarchy, gross ignorance, peremptory statements, and fantastical rumors sprinkled throughout this witness to a European intellect whose universal legacy is curiosity for the world and care for others. And so we find: "The inhabitants of Sierra Leone are not completely Negro black, but they have a very evil smell";[4] or, the Javanese are "thieving, spiteful and slavish";[5] or, the Tatars of Dagestan are "the ugliest of all and arch-robbers";[6] "Lapps" have "pointed chins and are just as sluggish as [they are] cowardly";[7] the Hottentots are so dirty that "they can all be smelled from a long way off," particularly because "they rub their newly born children with cow-dung and lay them in the sun."[8] In short, "Humanity has its highest degree of perfection in the white race. The yellow Indians have a somewhat lesser talent. The Negroes are much lower."[9]

Getting it right once is no guarantee for the future, and Kant offers a case in point. For this is the same philosopher who in the heart of Europe would proclaim the universality of rights, which is our focus now in this hour of perils: "A violation of rights in *one* part of the world is felt *everywhere*."[10] These are practically the final words of "Perpetual Peace," that essay by Kant whose publication in 1795 was the first enunciation of a "cosmopolitan right," which is the basis for "universal hospitality."[11] "One" and "every" proceed together: there are no rights for me that do not also belong to others; there is no people that is not accountable for the fate of other peoples.

And here we arrive at the central tension and contradiction that Europe must resolve if it is to avoid returning to square one—which is to say, privileges based on birth and origin, hierarchies among human beings, and the war of civilizations. As an abstract proclamation, the equality of rights demands a constant displacement in our practical lives, producing the endless discovery of new emancipations. It forces us to think against ourselves, to escape our rigidities and our conservatisms. It forces us to move, to accept the unexpected, to open ourselves to the unforeseen. Inviting us to an infinity of questions, this proclamation is simultaneously uncomfortable and boundless. By destabilizing what exists, it helps construct what is possible. All of which implies that, for it to come true, it must necessarily be collective, located in the patient apprenticeship of solidarities and brotherhoods, through active participation in the struggle for shared causes of equality. In other words, through new alliances derived from experience and from encountering the Other.

Those who hang on to an intangible reality, who benefit from their situations, their powers, and their dominations, are always going to fear the irrepressible promise of equality. What is new for our time is that despite our mobilization and resistance, the radical adversaries of equality are advancing. "That multiplicity of sickly characters" is how Antonio Gramsci (1891–1937) diagnosed their ancestors, the Italian fascists and the German National Socialists, when they began to dominate the scene between the two world wars of the last century.[12] Albeit in a different context today, their contemporary heirs have resumed the work of destruction that the defeat of the fascists in 1945 temporarily interrupted. Leading the charge of an old world that dies in the face of a new world that is slow to be born, they strive to end the era that began more than two centuries ago in France with the Declaration of the Rights of Man and of the Citizen, which states in its first article that "Men are born and remain free and equal in rights. Social distinctions can only be based on the common utility." A handful of words that forever take their stand against those whom Aimé Césaire called "the assassins of dawn."[13]

Kant, the peerless contemporary of that 1789 declaration, was born and died in Königsberg, a city which he never left. Königsberg is today known as Kaliningrad, located in Kaliningrad Oblast, a Russian enclave of one million inhabitants stuck between Lithuania and Poland. At the time I write these lines, its governor is a man by the name of Anton Alikhanov, a stalwart ally of Vladimir Putin, and a member of Putin's party and regime. Speaking in February 2024, during a forum of political scientists, held in a place that ought to be renamed for the Philosopher of the Enlightenment, Alikhanov took direct aim at Kant, making him responsible for all the chaos of our world in a tirade that repeats all the political grammar of Putinism:[14]

"I want to show that Immanuel Kant, born here some three hundred years ago, has a more or less direct connection to the global chaos that confronts us today. What's more, he has a direct connection to the military conflict in Ukraine." Why, you ask? Because he is "one of the founding fathers of the modern West," which is marked by "impiety and the absence of superior values." Alikhanov goes on to make Kant "the father of nearly everything": "He is the father of freedom, of the idea of the rule of law, of liberalism, of rationalism, and even the European Union. Some even say that the idea of the United Nations comes from him."

If we had any doubt about it, we have here the full list of what Vladimir Putin intends to tear down: the hope for a shared world of solidarity, equality, and the universality of rights. It's precisely this internationalist hope that for so long has implicated the persistent injustice suffered by the Palestinian people through Israel's obstinate denial of international law. A denial that has been carried to the point of nihilism by the extremist ruling coalition of Benjamin Netanyahu, who in January 2024 declared, "No one will arrest us. Not The Hague [seat of the global juridical proceedings, the International Court of Justice, and the International Criminal Court], not the Axis of Evil, not anyone else... This is the war of the children of light against the children of darkness." This is the same discourse maintained by Vladimir Putin and his ideologues with regard to Ukraine when they proclaim their determination to fight until victory in a "vital" war, one based on civilizational and identitarian grounds.

Fragile and imperfect though it may turn out to be, the conceptual leap of an international law that would apply to all nations was taken in 1945, after tragedy engendered the conviction that denying such a law is what covered the world in darkness. Moreover, this law must be equitable, not subject to a double standard. From this point of view, although the Bruges speech had been conceived as standing up to Russia, in the context of the war in Ukraine likened by Josep Borrell to the return of the "law of the jungle," that speech turned out to be an un-expected gift for Russian diplomacy from the European Union. Sergey Lavrov, Russia's unflappable minister of foreign affairs for more than twenty years after a decade spent at the United Nations, was not slow to take advantage. The metaphor of the civilized garden and the barbaric jungle now feeds the propaganda of the new imperial Russia that is confronting this "collective West," which Russia designates as its open enemy. By setting up the West as a symbol of decadence where, under the cover of democracy, traditional values and the hallmarks of identity are lost, Russia intends to rally the resentments of the rest of the world and assert itself as the protective power for a new order, both authoritarian and reactionary.[15]

"The West still believes that it is superior to everybody else," declared Lavrov on September 23, 2023, before the United Nations General Assembly in New York, commenting on this "notorious statement made by EU diplomacy chief Josep Borrell," according to which "Europe is a blooming garden, while everything around is a jungle." Lavrov's next blow came on October 10, 2023, in a written text broadcast by his ministry: "This is…pure colonialism." Assailing the Bruges speech as "Western exceptionalism…epitomized," he goes on to explain how "The collective West constantly violates the fundamental principle of non-interference in other countries' internal affairs."

Since then, when confronted with the war waged by Israel against Gaza after the massacres of October 7, 2023, the stance of the United States and its principal European allies—particularly Germany and France—has only bolstered the Russian argument by confirming the existence of a Western double standard that wreaks havoc on international law. With the war firmly entrenched in Ukraine—where, like Gaza, civilians are the primary victims—and with the Putin regime profiting from it to put a definitive end to all possibility of dissent in Russia, this inconsistency comes at a steep price. To support the war of Israel against Gaza, a war of conquest that extends to the occupied West Bank, is in a way to offer Russia its victory in Europe.

Not only do they share the same register of identitarian ideology that belongs to the far right, Russian president Vladimir Putin and Israeli prime minister Benjamin Netanyahu are also fighting for the same goal: the advent of a world with no law but force. International law, as they understand it, is nothing but respect for the sovereignty of states, including when those states violate fundamental rights, oppress other peoples, trample liberties, and commit crimes. The sole principle of liberty that Sergey Lavrov mentioned in his speech in New York in September 2023 was that of the "sovereign equality" between member states of the United Nations, which is articulated in Article 2 of the 1945 UN charter. There was no reference, on the other hand, to the Universal Declaration of Human Rights, adopted in Paris three years later, on December 10, 1948, which articulates "equal and inalienable rights" of "all members of the human family," and which affirms that those rights are "the foundation of liberty, justice, and peace in the world." Human rights, enforceable against states, no matter who they are.

The credibility of international law depends upon respecting this "no matter who they are." From Ukraine to Palestine, the message is as clear as it is distressing: the same Western powers that unanimously stood against the Russian invasion have chosen to abandon the Gazan population to their tragic fate. Judging by a ravaged Gaza and a murdered Palestine, where is the garden, and where is the jungle? Where have those gardeners gone, those European officials who have now abandoned the care of the world and of humanity? Far from being something foreign to us, the jungle flourishes through the blindness of conquest and power, of exploitation and domination. The garden, meanwhile, no matter how clean it looks, can be the soil of worse barbarities, which, in the name of supposedly superior identities, origins, and civilizations, lead to the crime of genocide.

Look now at two reports, separated by two years, sharing an identical title: "The Court indicates provisional measures." The first, from March 16, 2022, regards Ukraine; the second, from January 26, 2024, relates to Gaza. In both cases, the International Court of Justice, the principal judicial organ of the United Nations, of which all member states are ipso facto members, enacts an ordinance regarding two of these states, which the court defines as binding. In 2022, in terse prose, it enjoined Russia to "immediately suspend the military operations that began on February 24, 2022, within the territory of Ukraine." In 2024, in detailed prose, it enjoined Israel to "take all measures in its power to prevent the commission against the Palestinians of Gaza of all acts within the scope" of the Convention on the Prevention and Punishment of the Crime of Genocide.

Neither Russia nor Israel is subject to the requirements of the International Court of Justice, even though Article 94 of the United Nations Charter stipulates that "Each member of the United Nations undertakes to comply with the decision of the Court of International Justice in any case to which it is a party." That charter, adopted on June 26, 1945, just as the Second World War was ending, begins with these words: "We the peoples of the United Nations determined to save succeeding generations from the scourge of war, which twice in our lifetime has brought untold sorrow to mankind, to reaffirm faith in the fundamental human rights, in the dignity and worth of the human person, in the equal rights of men and women and of nations, large and small…"

This is obviously not the first time, nor, alas, will it be the last, when states blithely and with impunity violate international law, which they nevertheless appeal to when it suits them. But without a doubt, it is the first time that the simultaneous existence of two wars, which threaten devastating consequences for peace in the entire world, has placed before the eyes of all people the cynical hypocrisy of nations that lay claim to the universal, the right, the just, and the good.

It is an incontestable fact that the current leaders of France, Europe, and the United States have granted different weight to international law depending on whether it relates to the fate of the Ukrainian people or that of the Palestinian people. Faced with the Russian aggression against Ukraine, we have a veritable deluge of diplomatic retaliations, economic sanctions, and military support. Faced with a war of extermination by Israel against the Gazan population—with the massacre of civilians, particularly of infants, the destruction of an entire society, the ravages of famine, and this obvious crime against humanity in order to drive the Palestinians from their land—we see only vague appeals for restraint and overdue humanitarian actions. But no stop to the fighting. Indeed, far from it, since the

Israeli army has continued to benefit from Western aid, including military, and unfailing support from the United States of America.

In short, international law brooks no distinctions. We cannot support the Ukrainian people while abandoning the Palestinian people. Just as we cannot defend the Palestinian cause while deserting the Ukrainian cause. In both cases, the same principles are at stake, and those principles lose all value if they are open to double standards. Only this commitment can construct a bulwark against Vladimir Putin and everyone like him, against the threat, not only imperialist but also fascist, that he embodies.[16] Yet with regard to Gaza, that principle has been dramatically disavowed.

International law is the entire scaffold of rules, principles, and values that was erected above states and nations when the shock of the European catastrophe and its incommensurable crimes produced the sudden realization that we cannot rely on individual nation-states to guarantee the peace of the world. Just as the proclamation of a natural equality of rights does not automatically produce actual equality, this international law comes into effect before it becomes reality. It is a rigorous standard, a care for humanity, a horizon of the universal. It is an old promise made to the world by Europe. If Europe itself breaks this promise, betrays it utterly, that does nothing to diminish its subversive force.

Over more than two centuries, how many Bastilles throughout the world have been stormed by the equality of rights, including in France, the very nation which prides itself on having proclaimed that concept? Even Kant sensed this endless shaking of oppressive powers that think themselves immutable, if we are to believe the anecdote, endlessly repeated, of the philosopher making a rare interruption to his ritual of a daily walk on July 15, 1789, upon hearing the announcement of the Bastille being captured the previous night in Paris.

A mere six weeks later, on August 26, 1789, the brand-new National Assembly adopted the Declaration of the Rights of Man and of the Citizen. The proclamation was entirely unimaginable. By affirming equality, it decreed a humanity without division, without distinction based on birth, without hierarchy based on origin. Its first words identified respect for rights as the condition of public happiness and the integrity of leaders: "The representatives of the French people, constituted in a National Assembly, and considering that being ignorant of, forgetting, or disregarding the rights of man are the sole causes of public misfortunes and the corruption of governments, have resolved to set forth, in a solemn declaration, the natural, inalienable, and sacred rights of man."

"*Ah! ça ira, ça ira, ça ira…*" That was the chorus of a famous revolutionary song that burst onto the scene in Paris in the spring of 1790. The ideals of equality had the advantage that every citadel seemed powerless to resist them, and "Oh! It will be okay" was the motto of this unwavering optimism.

> *Oh! It will be okay, it will be okay, it will be okay*
> *The people today never cease to say*
> *Oh! It will be okay, it will be okay, it will be okay*
> *Despite the mutineers, all will succeed*
> *Our enemies, dismayed, go on standing there*
> *And we will sing, "Hallelujah!"*

The chorus of this popular song came to France as a legacy from America, where memory recalls that the aspiration to an equal humanity had no flag, identity card, or nation. "*Ça ira, ça ira,*" was Benjamin Franklin's invariable reply, in his halting French, when people asked him for news of the war for American independence when he represented in Paris, from 1776 to 1785, the Congress of the thirteen British colonies in North America. A reasonable optimism that he took from the truth that equality, because it is obvious, will necessarily win. It is formulated in those terms in the American Declaration of Independence, ratified on July 4, 1776: "We hold these truths to be self-evident, that all men are created equal, that they are endowed by their Creator with certain unalienable Rights, that among these are Life, Liberty and the pursuit of Happiness. That to secure these rights, Governments are instituted among Men, deriving their just powers from the consent of the governed."

"Oh, it will be okay!" It is not certain that we are able, today, to offer ourselves the luxury of that overpowering optimism. For in truth, things are not going very well. In the United States as well as in Europe, the determined adversaries of equal rights are coming back in force. Not only aiming at power, they go on to obtain it. Their initial targets are immigrants, foreigners, women, Muslims, minorities with regard to appearance, religion, or race, sexual orientation or gender identity, etc. In the end, no slice of humanity will escape their violence so long as their ultimate goal aims at the very principle of equal rights. Which at its core is the right to have rights.[17]

For at the most basic level, a single human right sums them all up: the right to have rights at all. To have them and to keep them, to demand them and to win them.

3 ▸ THEIR HATRED OF EQUALITY

"WITH PÉTAIN, WE COULD emerge from the tunnel of 1789." So writes Charles Maurras (1868–1952) in the years following the Second World War, recalling the summer of 1940, when Philippe Pétain became prime minister of the Vichy government in France, which surrendered the name as well as the ideals of the French Republic. Maurras was an emblematic figure of Action Française, the preeminent military movement of the modern far right, which was founded in 1899 and embraced the infernal logic of exclusion. By defining Protestants, Jews, Freemasons, and immigrants as "four confederate states" that formed "Anti-France," Maurras theorized a radical rejection of the diverse and the elsewhere, the different and the dissident. It is the same rejection that we see, once again, in the stigmatization of minorities and pluralities by a resurgent fascism today.

And so the birth of the French Republic in 1789, a moment we see as a dawn full of promise, was for Maurras a night that ended only in 1940, when an imperfect republican democracy committed suicide, and its most tenacious enemies triumphed. Under an exterior that has subsequently been toned down and dressed up, the far right of today has not changed its agenda. Nor has there been any change in the political interests in France, particularly economic, that lend them a hand, preferring to be governed by identitarian racists, not egalitarian socialists.

If the following review of past figures and events appears to presage the political polemics and media manipulations of the legislative elections in 2024—when President Emmanuel Macron arbitrarily chose a chaotic dissolution of the French parliament—those parallels are not the product of historical chance. The circumstances are dissimilar, the contexts are disparate, the protagonists are different. But the ideological chords remain the same: panic felt by the wealthy, irrational fear toward the stranger, hatred for equality. The very things that are at stake here and now.

On October 16, 1936, a manifesto entitled "Four Months of the Popular Front" was simultaneously published by three hundred daily and weekly papers in and around Paris. Denouncing "a socialist government held prisoner by the communists" and delivered "into the hands of secretive powers that were preparing to Sovietize the country," it entreated "French people of all persuasions" to defend "French civilization" by fighting its "most treacherous and dangerous [enemy]: communism."

Two years later, on December 16, 1938, the journalistic community that initiated the first call to action, with the financial support of the business elite, launched a second manifesto under the title "An Appeal of 430 French Newspapers." Expressing support for the Munich Agreement that was signed two months earlier, which marked the Franco-British abdication to Nazi Germany, the signatories demanded that parliament dissolve the Communist Party because "it is the most powerful, the most active, and the most dangerous of the foreign factions to gain a foothold upon our soil."

Behind these two initiatives is the same forgotten individual and a little-known history that goes straight to the heart of the media's collaboration with the occupying Nazis. Namely, Dominique Sordet, a music critic and follower of Maurras who became a reactionary activist and would go on to create the Inter-France Agency. At a time when the influence of the press over public opinion was immense, comparable to that of mass-media conglomerates today, Inter-France used the support of the business community to rapidly become the largest operation for the manipulation of public opinion. Under the Occupation, Inter-France went on to mold the press to the interests of Hitler in occupied France as well as the Vichy regime in the so-called Free Zone.

In his book *L'Agence Inter-France de Pétain à Hitler* [The Inter-France Agency: from Pétain to Hitler], Gérard Bonet has documented the lightning rise of Inter-France. Nationalist at its inception, it became Pétainist, then openly collaborationist, before finishing as plainly Hitlerian.[1] Bonet's work lifts the curtain on an episode, largely ignored by historians, that demonstrates the French debasement in the middle of the last century: the moment when journalism surrendered to the business world and defended their interests, abandoning the pursuit of information in exchange for the hegemony of beliefs—and in this case, the most hateful beliefs.

Dominique Sordet, who would not be put on trial by the Liberation because he died in hiding in March 1946, left behind a testament in the form of a book that shines a harsh light on the ideological domain of the far right that was gathered around him. Published in June 1944, at a time when all would soon be lost for him and his world, *The Last Days of Democracy* contains an address given before the intellectual elite of the Collaboration on the preceding March 25.[2] In it, Sordet identifies "the equality of all people" as the ideology that, ever since Jean-Jacques Rousseau and the French Revolution, "has ruled over civilized nations," causing their "organic decline."

This short work has the merit of extreme candor that is echoed in our present moment, in which the far right has the wind in its sails while it asserts the identity of peoples, nations, and states as a means to destroy the universality of rights. "What is democracy?" asks Sordet, before answering his own question: "The doctrinaires of democracy propose a first principle, which is the equality of all people." And that is where he puts his cards on the table: "The democratic state descends from Judaism. Equality is a Jewish passion. As the polar opposite of the egalitarian spirit, the notion of hierarchy is, on the contrary, essentially Aryan."

Written in 1944, this ideological and murderous—never forget!—delirium underscores the political stakes of the current battle, which must be fought without reserve or the least ambiguity, against anti-Semitism: "To a high degree," wrote this French musicologist turned fascist, "Israel has spread the venom of egalitarian passion throughout all civilizations marked by its fingerprints." By blaming Judaism for the spread of equality, Sordet's words confirm that for the anti-Semite, hatred of Jews is nothing other than hatred of man, that is, of a humanity united around the universal promise of equality. This mediocre essay thus turns the "egalitarian passion" into the source of all evils, with democracy as its poisonous fruit, which must be destroyed because it rests on the harmful illusion that "every man is worth any other." Describing his historic moment as the "end of a myth that is dissolving in a bloody twilight," Sordet speaks the plain truth of the far right.

What is the far right? Quite simply, it is the hatred of equality. What sets it apart from conservative or reactionary parties, politics, and leaders is the radicalness of its ideological foundation. If, behind its new sheen of respectability, the far right is often physically violent in its militant actions, if it is explicitly racist and xenophobic in its slogans, taking foreigners and dual citizens as its first targets, if it stands in clear opposition to the rights of women and sexual minorities in its manifestoes, that is because it is moved by an ancient wish for a revenge against what is the essential principle of every democracy, however imperfectly that principle may be applied.

Because democracy does not consist only of elections, which might be nothing more than a sham, as we see, for example, in the neofascist Russia of Vladimir Putin, that powerful backer of the European and North American far right. To reduce democracy to the vote is to weaken it and allow it to be destroyed from within by some elected power. No, stripped to its origin and its roots, democracy is a promise, never fully achieved, eternally rebegun, ceaselessly updated: that of equal rights. And this equality, which was proclaimed in the Declaration of the Rights of Man and of the Citizen (1789) and extended in the Universal Declaration of Human Rights (1948), is what has paved the way for countless emancipations by ceaselessly inviting the abolition of privileges, dominations, and oppressions, including against powers born from earlier emancipatory struggles or those who claim that mantle.

Fragile and incomplete, all our social and democratic triumphs flow from that principle of equality—including victories won against those who see themselves as heirs and guardians of equality, even as they promote colonial or patriarchal interests with an untroubled conscience. The right of peoples to self-determination, like the right of women over their own bodies and lives, underlines the inexhaustible vitality of this horizon of hope. Equal rights, without distinction, is the principle that rejects an intangible form of house arrest whereby human beings are made prisoners of their birth, condition, origin, appearance, belief, sex, or gender.

The emancipatory movement of that principle has kept on tearing down the perverse mechanism of the outcast and the upstart, by which those who win their rights go on to slam the door in the face of those next in line. Yesterday, this was the pioneering battle of the Haitian antislavery revolution, taking down owners who were freethinkers even while they disdained the humanity of the slaves. Today, it is the pioneering battle of #MeToo, which does not stop at equality in work, family, and politics, but shakes up that former feminism by going on to declare war upon centuries of masculine domination in private life, including sexual relations, which spans all social spheres. Next, it is the upcoming battle of radical ecology that reminds the human race that its inventiveness does not give it a right to prey upon the infinity of life on the planet.

Joining forces against the far right—which managed to keep them out of power in the French legislative elections of 2024—is therefore not only a tactical electoral strategy but also a vital political necessity. To grant them the reins of power would be to open a hellish Pandora's box. Because what all the currents of the far right have in common—with their diverse intellectual, activist, and electoral variants—is the desire to overthrow the citadel of human rights, undermining their foundation of natural equality and disrupting their universal application. The doctrine that unites the far right can be summed up as the denial of any shared humanity or free individual.

The following claim appears inoffensive, but we know how bloody its consequences were, given that European history embraced it along the road to genocides and crimes against humanity: "The main plank in the National Socialist program is to abolish the liberalistic concept of the individual and the Marxist concept of humanity and to substitute therefore the folk community, rooted in the soil and bound together by the bond of its common blood. A very simple statement; but it involves a principle that has tremendous consequences."[3] These words come from Adolf Hitler, in a speech delivered on January 30, 1937, in the German Reichstag. In other words, only what is good for Germany and its people—and for them alone—is right. This had been his credo ever since he wrote *Mein Kampf* in prison in 1924–25, which was published in Germany as early as 1925. Unfortunately, the political left of that time, the socialists and the communists, were lost in their fratricidal wars and failed to see the devastating significance of this denial of free will and universal equality.

Having been warned, we cannot allow ourselves the luxury of underestimating the current danger, naively believing that if the far right comes to power, they would merely extend what the political right is already doing. Especially when the political right persists in making common cause with the far right, looking for allies in the fight to preserve the interests of the dominant class, who form the "icy water of egotistic calculation,"[4] as Karl Marx perceived so early, and whose decisive role is remembered by Éric Vuillard in *The Order of the Day*, a novel that surveys Hitler's ascent to power in 1933.[5] As we see not only in Russia and Hungary, but also in India, now the most populus country on the planet, caught in the net of a supremacist Hindu power—as happened in Poland and in Brazil, as will be the case if Donald Trump regains the presidency of the United States, and as is currently taking place in Italy with Giorgia Meloni: when the far right reaches the summit of governmental and state apparatuses, a devastating gyre is always unleashed upon equality and universal rights.

The method of the far right is to anchor itself to the long ideological tradition of rejecting those democratic ideals that the French Revolution inaugurated and continues to symbolize. As documented by the historian Zeev Sternhell,[6] many of these "anti-Enlightenment" thinkers in Europe are French—though Francophone may be more correct, since the first of these counterrevolutionary thinkers, Joseph de Maistre (1753–1821), was a Savoyard in the years before Savoy was annexed by France. This Savoyard, whose statue still stands in the very center of the city of Chambéry, was also the guest of the czar's empire, living in Russia for fourteen long years as minister plenipotentiary for the kingdom of Sardinia.

The founder of Action Française, Charles Maurras, drank from this spring, referring to Maistre as "the first of our political philosophers." So did the Nazi legal scholar Carl Schmitt (1888–1985), so much so that philosopher Isaiah Berlin describes Maistre as a "a kind of precursor and early preacher of Fascism."[7] In effect, the work of Joseph de Maistre laid the foundation for the ideology that buttresses the far right today: the denial of a common humanity and the rejection of the principle of equality.

According to Maistre, man does not have inherent rights qua man, as he claims in a famous passage from his *Considerations on France*. Criticizing a political moment when the French Revolution regained momentum after the Thermidorian Reaction, Maistre writes, "The Constitution of 1795, like its predecessors, was made for *man*. But there is no such thing as *man* in the world. In my lifetime, I have seen Frenchmen, Italians, Russians, etc.; thanks to Montesquieu, I even know that *one can be Persian*. But as for *man*, I declare that I have never in my life met him; if he exists, he is unknown to me."[8] On the other hand, this particular man excels at being the kind that denigrates women: "A woman can only be superior as a woman; as soon as she wants to emulate man, she is nothing but an ape."[9]

This hierarchy of humanity is joined to a radically antidemocratic theory of power: "If the governed many can believe themselves equal to the small number who govern, there will be no more government."[10] It is no coincidence that the Italian anti-Mafia magistrate Roberto Scarpinato summarizes Maistre's ideas in his *Il ritorno del principe* [The return of the prince], considering them to be the quintessential theorization of a domination that is built upon the blindness of its subjects: "Power must exist beyond the comprehension of the mob of the governed. Authority must constantly be preserved from criticism through the psychological instruments of religion, patriotism, tradition, and prejudice."[11] Maistre's words foreshadow mass media, television, radio, and digital networks that spread the far right's views throughout the public sphere, killing the truth of facts under a mantle of freedom of speech, smothering information under the dictatorship of opinions, and in short ushering in the reign of lies.

Far from being forgotten, Joseph de Maistre is still read, recommended, and commented upon by the far right. "Joseph de Maistre: The Right of Nations Against the Rights of Man" is a title from the May 2023 edition of *Éléments*, the journal of the Research and Study Group for European Civilization (GRECE). An intellectual circle as sophisticated as it is radical, GRECE has, since its creation in 1969, been a faithful midwife to the rebirth of the European far right. Its counterpart in Russia, which publishes a Russian version of *Éléments*, is none other than Aleksandr Dugin, a neofascist and ultranationalist ideologue who under Vladimir Putin has become a zealous propagandist for Russian imperialism and its military expansion.

The article in *Éléments* is an interview with Marc Froidefont, an expert on the thought of the reactionary Savoyard monarchist. According to Froidefont, "The Declaration of the Rights of Man is the vehicle for an ideology that is lethal to traditional nations, and Joseph de Maistre was one of the first to sound the alarm." He also states, "Joseph de Maistre's critique of human rights is more relevant than ever. It is in the name of this celebrated declaration in 1789 that European nations are today threatened with death. That which is privileged in this declaration is man in the abstract. As a result, some laws have been passed that condemn anybody who dares remind us that a nation belongs, first and foremost, to the heirs of those who patiently constructed it, over hundreds of years, with their sweat and their blood."[12]

If anyone might doubt that, under the academic polish of these words, racism and xenophobia are being called forth into action, and even used to drive out those of us who are not the aforementioned "heirs," the same interview cites Maistre's Islamophobia with approval. According to Maistre, Froidefont explains, "conflict between Christianity and Islam is inevitable. His views are unambiguous when he writes, 'War between us and them is natural, peace the reverse. As soon as the Christian and the Mussulman come in contact, the one or the other must yield or perish.'"[13]

Gazing in shock at the horrors that abound in the mass media taken over by the far right, it is easy to forget that such awfulness is not the product of an excessive radicality, but that it emerges from the very heart of its ideology and is passed around by intellectuals with degrees and titles. Accompanying the shift of the old republican right toward the far right, *Le Figaro*, official newspaper of the French right,[14] recently promoted *Les Mensonges de l'égalité* [The lies of equality], the work of another academic, the law professor Jean-Louis Harouel.[15] Forty years ago, this author wrote *Essai sur l'inégalité* [Essay on inequality], though its impact at that time was marginal. "Equality is a mortal danger for the West," writes Harouel today. "It is like a poison that kills it."

Laying into "the ideology formed by a symbiosis of wokeism and human-rightsmanship, in close association with environmentalism," Harouel does not hesitate to affirm that "the religion of equality reveals itself to be still more dangerous than was communism." He states, "In the name of equality, communism was a deadly secular religion that tormented all who submitted to it, though without making them disappear; the lunacy of equality, however, which inspires the religion of human rights, does nothing more nor less than pave the way for the annihilation of European peoples." The example that comes next to his pen is "the concrete equality between women and men," to which he attributes "the demographic collapse of the nations of Europe."

In an older work, *Human Rights Against the People*, which came out in 2016, the same author calls on us "once again to make self-love a priority," as opposed to "the insane universalism of the religion of human rights that claims immigration to be a new human right."[16] And so "it is essential to discriminate," Harouel theorizes, before making a recommendation "to subject Islam to a particular status" in order to let Muslims know that "France, in none of its parts, is a territory of Islam." By way of conclusion, this professor emeritus of the University of Panthéon-Assas in Paris writes, "France cannot hope to survive unless it renounces its state religion of human rights."

Among all our various sensibilities, engagements, and positions, this is a truth that we must look full in the face, everywhere in the world, but particularly in Europe, on the continent where these ideas were first proclaimed: any victory for the far right is not simply the worsening of the conservative politics already at work. Rather, it would mark a historic rupture by allowing the avowed adversaries of our common humanity and our individual free will to take their revenge. To pave the way, to accept that risk, to accommodate the far right in any way would mean empowering extremists who oppose equality, deny universal humanity, and take their stand against the fundamental principles of human rights.[17]

4 ▸ TURNING THE WORLD UPSIDE DOWN

TO IMAGINE THE GARDEN is also to imagine nature without people.

In a manifesto that he published online before committing his Islamophobic massacre that claimed fifty-one lives in two mosques in the New Zealand city of Christchurch on March 15, 2019, the Australian terrorist of the far right, Brenton Tarrant, proclaimed a kind of ecofascism: an exterminating racism with the ultimate goal of saving nature. "The environment is being destroyed by overpopulation, and we Europeans are the only ones who are not contributing to overpopulation" he wrote, before proclaiming this mandate: "We must kill the invaders, kill overpopulation, and in doing so save the environment."[1]

The historian Guillaume Blanc, a specialist on contemporary Africa, does not hesitate to make the following reminder in his study of "green colonialism," in which the well-meaning curiosity of Western tourists is complicit. "The more that nature disappears in the West, the more we fantasize about it in Africa," explains Blanc, who recounts how, starting from the distant origins of colonialism and continuing with contemporary environmental projects, a "naturalization of large areas of the continent" of Africa has been carried out. "By naturalization," he explains, "I am referring to the dehumanization of Africa, a process which involves turning territories into parks, banning agriculture in these areas, evicting people from their homes and getting rid of their fields and grazing land in order to create a supposedly natural world where people are absent. And this battle for a phantom Africa has no impact whatsoever on the destruction of biodiversity. On the contrary, this process is proving to have disastrous effects on all those living in the natural world. The forced eviction of local people, fines, prison sentences, social breakdown, beatings, sometimes rape and even murders: these are the catastrophic consequences of this westernized vision of Africa."[2]

This ideal of African nature protected from Africans themselves traces a continuity between the past of colonial empires and the present of international agencies: from the "civilizational duty of the white man" to the "ecological burden of the Western expert," "the intention may no longer be the same, but the spirit remains identical: the modern and civilized world must continue to save Africa from the Africans."[3] This detour carries us back to where the Bruges speech lost its way: by imposing a hierarchy of values, in which wild nature is inferior to nature that has been mastered, the metaphor of garden and jungle loses touch with care for humanity. And by essentializing this opposition between two worlds, it does more than distinguish them or differentiate them: it establishes a separation.

Separation is the meaning of apartheid, the Afrikaans word that is partially derived from the French phrase *à part*. Inaugurated in South Africa starting in 1948, apartheid imposed a racist policy of "separate development," which discriminated against and separated the Black and mixed-race populations for the benefit of the white population of European ancestry. Apartheid ended only in 1991, even though, ever since a 1973 resolution of the United Nations, it was considered a crime under international law. The invention of apartheid, which descended from colonial policies of segregation, was nothing less than a modern radicalization of those policies. The appearance of apartheid in 1948, the same year as the adoption of the Universal Declaration of Human Rights, confirms that a full reckoning of the causes of the European catastrophe had not been achieved. Grand

principles were proclaimed, yet at the same time forgotten, by an officially racist state that would long
benefit from Western support and indulgence, until
such time as people became outraged and called for
a boycott of South Africa.

Our gardens, then, which are actually jungles:
the invention of apartheid took the baton from
Auschwitz, stopping short of mass extermination
but continuing to negate human beings through exclusion, sorting, and erasure. A legacy of European
colonialism, this state-sanctioned racism preserved
the criminal ideology that was at the origin of the
genocide of the Jews of Europe, keeping it alive as a
constantly active principle. It would take more than
four decades to bring an end to apartheid. And this
achievement was not, predominantly, the work of
the West and its powers but rather of its victims and
their resistance, embodied primarily in Nelson Mandela, who paid the heavy price of twenty-seven years
in prison.

Africa reminds Europe of its inconsistency: it is
by losing its humanity in Africa that Europe comes
home and goes astray on its own continent. In 1948,
Namibia became part of South Africa until its independence in 1990. But it is in Namibia that the
first genocide of the twentieth century took place.
Between 1904 and 1908, when it was a German colony, the Herero and Nama peoples were victims of

a policy of extermination in massive numbers. This genocide was carried out under the orders of General Lothar von Trotha, notably the author of this order, signed on October 2, 1904: "All the Herero must leave the country. If they do not, I will force them to do so with my cannons. Every Herero discovered within the limits of German territory, armed or unarmed, with or without livestock, will be shot. I will not take any more women or children. They must go back to their people or let themselves be shot. These are my words to the Herero people."

The world remembers when we forget. In light of the inaction of Europe and its North American projection, it is South Africa that stepped forward to defend the universality of human rights when faced with the destruction of Palestine by Israel. At the beginning of 2024, its petition before the UN's International Court of Justice (ICJ) against the State of Israel for the "genocidal nature" of its war against the Palestinians of Gaza was not only an unprecedented legal event, but it also marked a geopolitical reversal: at a time when all the peoples of the world observed, through the Palestinian tragedy, the double standard applied by Europe and the United States to the universal values that they profess, it was South Africa, a country emblematic of emancipatory, anti-colonial, and anti-racist causes in the Third World, that took up the torch.

Reading the incredible document produced by the South African diplomatic corps, and listening on January 11, 2024, to the oral presentation of their arguments before the ICJ, forces us to grapple with the intellectual eclipse of a continent, our own, where nation-states have for so long claimed to articulate, codify, and impose the good, the just, and the true.

Yet in real time and under the gaze of the entire world, when faced with the martyrdom of Gaza, those nation-states said nothing, nothing beyond several hypocritical calls for restraint. And they did nothing—or worse than nothing, when they performed the opposite of that restraint and followed the example of the United States by delivering massive amounts of weapons and ammunition to Israel. Nothing said and nothing done while the population of one of the most densely populated territories on the planet was attacked by one of the most powerful armies in the world, after a siege and occupation, in one of the most intensive bombing campaigns of modern military history. Worse than Aleppo in Syria, worse than Mariupol in Ukraine, to refer to two contemporary examples for which Russia is to blame, but also worse, in proportional intensity, than the Allied bombardments of Nazi Germany.

Through the actions of its army as much as the words of its leaders, an entire people has been targeted by Israel's vengeful retaliation for the terrorist attack and the massacre of Israeli citizens carried out by Hamas on October 7, 2023. Far from a proportionate response, this retaliation is an indiscriminate punishment carried out against an entire population by reason of their origin, their identity, their culture, and their history.

It is the Palestinian people of Gaza—and by extension the very idea of a viable Palestine, of a life and an existence under that name, with all the social interaction and citizenship that would entail—who were defined as culpable and must be indiscriminately punished. This message was conveyed explicitly, from the first day, by the Israeli prime minister Benjamin Netanyahu himself, who called for a holy war by referring to Amalek, the people that God orders in the Bible to be exterminated: "You will spare none of them, and you will put to death men and women, children and infants, cows and sheep, camels and donkeys" (1 Samuel 15:3).

In just the first three months of the war, the number of dead, missing, and wounded was already in the tens of thousands, mainly civilians, the majority of whom were children and women. An entire world destroyed forever: homes and hospitals, places of living and of faith, schools and universities, government offices, stores, monuments, libraries, even cemeteries. "Nowhere is safe in Gaza," the secretary-general of the United Nations did not hesitate to affirm on

December 6, 2023, in a somber letter to the Security Council. Since then, humanitarian NGOs and UN agencies have not stopped warning of polluted water, the spread of famine, immeasurable misery and infinite despair—in short, the destruction beyond all repair of a part of occupied Palestine.

What a grim reversal! The state whose initial legitimacy was based on the awareness of the crime of genocide committed against the Jews by the Nazis and their allies is today facing the accusation of reproducing that crime against the Palestinians. The Convention of 1948 that was invoked by South Africa defines the crime of genocide as certain actions "committed with intent to destroy, in whole or in part, a national, ethnical, racial or religious group, as such." Raphael Lemkin, the inventor of the word—taken from *genos* in Greek and *cide* in Latin—defines it as "a conspiracy to exterminate a national, religious, or racial group."[4]

Beyond the horror it cannot fail to provoke, the war to annihilate Palestine carried out by the State of Israel justifies a legal debate on its classification as genocide, which includes an evaluation of the intentions of Israeli leaders, confirmed by many of their statements. In any case, what was at stake in the emergency procedure before the ICJ was the need to interrupt, as quickly as possible, a process of obliteration, the purging and expelling, the erasure and destruction of the Palestinians in Gaza, actions which have genocidal characteristics and tragically recall the genocides committed in Rwanda in 1994 and in Bosnia in 1995. None of this is meant in any way to relativize the uniqueness of the Shoah, the deliberate plan by the Nazi regime for the mass extermination of millions of human beings in the Holocaust, but rather it is a call to maintain a universal vigilance against the repetition, in other contexts and in various forms, of this incommensurable crime of humanity against itself.

Sadly, history will record that the powers known collectively as the West, that political reality born from Europe's projection upon the world, in the very moment that they boasted of having proclaimed the universality of equal rights, shirked that vigilance by abandoning Palestine to its tragic fate. Through the audacity of South Africa, we can see that the people and nations who have been the victims of the West's hypocrisy have now made themselves the best defenders of the universal. In short, they remind Europe of the promise it has betrayed.

"If we wish to live up to our peoples' expectations, we must seek the response elsewhere than in Europe."[5] These are nearly the final words of *The Wretched of the Earth*, that essay by Frantz Fanon that ever since its publication in 1961 has circled the planet. Fanon's words can be read as a prediction of the reversal that today is being accomplished. This invitation to "change sides" represents an emancipatory turn in the quest for a true humanism, where care for humanity is not eclipsed by the interests of dominating nations or the identities of conquering peoples. In the wake of the *Discourse on Colonialism*, by Aimé Césaire,[6] Fanon's compatriot from Martinique, *The Wretched of the Earth* celebrates a true universalism, without a nation owning others, without identitarian borders.

"May I be allowed to discover and desire man wherever he may be,"[7] writes Fanon in the conclusion of his first book, *Black Skin, White Masks*, published in 1952, in which he recalls this warning from "[his] philosophy professor from the Antilles... 'When you hear someone insulting the Jews, pay attention; he is talking about you.'"[8] To which Fanon adds this commentary: "The anti-Semite is inevitably a negrophobe."[9] As the epigraph to one of the chapters, he selected these words by Aimé Césaire: "There is not in the world one single poor lynched bastard, one poor tortured man, in whom I am not also murdered and humiliated."[10]

International law is the legal translation of this fundamental humanism, the very humanism that Fanon, after ten years of French colonial wars, from Vietnam to Algeria, would furiously observe that Europe had rejected. "Leave this Europe," he writes in *The Wretched of the Earth*, "where they are never done talking of Man, yet murder men everywhere they find them, at the corner of every one of their own streets, in all the corners of the globe... Europe has declined all humility and all modesty; but she also set her face against all solicitude and tenderness. She has only shown herself parsimonious and niggardly where men are concerned; it is only men that she has killed and devoured. So, my brothers, how is it that we do not understand that we have better things to do than to follow that same Europe?"[11]

In this indictment, Fanon holds Europe up against itself, brandishing the betrayed promise to demand, finally, its fulfillment. This Europe, which proclaimed natural equality and then enacted the universality of rights, trampled and vandalized first the one and then the other through colonialism and imperialism, denying them to the populations of human beings that it was oppressing and exploiting. And it is this devastating duplicity that has been practiced up until the present day through the long injustice inflicted upon Palestine, in the occupation and colonization of its territories since 1967. The resulting segregation and discrimination against its people spread a poison within Israeli society that is fatal for democratic ideals, as demonstrated by the rise of Jewish forces of the far right, who are as racist as the anti-Semites.

The current resonance of Fanon's book-length manifesto proves that the internationalist and humanist hope of decolonization is not out of date, but is always a promise. Appearing several days before the death of its author, who married himself to the cause of Algerian independence, *The Wretched of the Earth* was published in 1961, the very year in which Nelson Mandela, renouncing the South African ANC's strategy of nonviolence in the face of the apartheid regime, traveled to receive training in armed struggle from the Algerian FLN at their secret bases in Morocco, a few months before his arrest on August 5, 1962. But the resonance goes yet further: apartheid, the regime of racial separation, was established in 1948, the same year that the United Nations gave its seal of approval to the creation of the State of Israel, promulgated the Universal Declaration of Human Rights, and ratified the Convention on the Prevention and Punishment of the Crime of Genocide.

To reread Frantz Fanon is thus to realize what is at stake for our future, in light of what Palestine has been saying to the world ever since its right to exist as an independent state was denied—even though Palestine, with Yasser Arafat, eventually conceded that right to the State of Israel, despite the expulsion that part of its people suffered in 1948 during the Nakba. Fanon's writings pose this question: Who today is going to preserve the universal and its promises of rights, justice, and equality? Who will keep these rights free from a predatory appropriation by states, peoples, and nations that claim to be the proper owners of a universal, believing themselves authorized to contradict it and flout it whenever their own self-interests—primarily economic—are in peril?

South Africa answered that question before the court in The Hague: there is no universal over which any particular nation, civilization, culture, and so on, possesses a monopoly or sole ownership. There is only the universalizable, which is at stake whenever the fate of a particular portion of humanity—attacked, persecuted, violated, discriminated against, erased, or exterminated—puts the fate of all humanity at risk. Rigorously juridical within the field of international law, the South African petition before the ICJ posed a politically momentous question: Do supranational values apply universally, without regard to borders—namely, those values that the European Union and the nation-states of our continent claim, at least on paper, to follow?

The essential principles, values, and rights that South Africa invoked in light of Israel's actions in Gaza do not apply only to Palestine. They apply equally to Ukraine, the victim of a Russian war of aggression and imperialism, with its heap of war crimes and crimes against humanity. But they also apply to the people of Syria, who are the martyrs, yesterday and today, of the dictatorial regime that oppresses them. Just as they apply for all peoples who suffer the yoke of state powers—from Iran to Turkey, not forgetting the absolute monarchies that rule in the Arabian Peninsula—that make a show of supporting the Palestinian cause to distract from the unjust fate they impose upon their own peoples.

"The cosmopolitan right must be guided by the conditions of universal hospitality," wrote Kant before asserting the inextricable ties between "one" and "all," between the fate of one people and that of every other. Truly, there is no humanism unless it is internationalist.

5 ▸ THE COLONIAL QUESTION

"ATAI!" WHENEVER I WALK through the Jardin des Plantes in Paris, I never fail to salute the spirit of Atai, who led the great Kanak revolt of 1878 in New Caledonia. Startling the strangers around me in the park, I cry out his name each time I pass the white elm that was planted in 2014, when France restored Atai's skull to his people, after hiding it away for so long in the repositories of the Museum of Natural History as the barbaric trophy of a colonial power.

Atai is not the only phantom that haunts this site of the ancient Jardin du Roi, established in 1635,[1] the same year that the French colonial adventure accelerated with the seizure of Martinique and Guadeloupe in the Lesser Antilles archipelago. Next came Saint-Domingue, which would become Haiti after the abolitionist revolution in 1804. As France gradually appropriated the western side of the large island of Hispaniola in the seventeenth century, Saint-Domingue became the jewel in its first colonial empire, a symbol of its dazzling wealth. Deported, sold, caged, chained, objectified, and exploited, the people who were enslaved and transported there from Africa became the human material governed by the Black Code, promulgated in 1685, which decreed the rules for using slaves, just as one might regulate the optimal use of any other raw material.

In recent years, out of the depository of the Museum of Natural History, which likewise supplies the Museum of Humanity in Paris, France restored the skulls of Maori warriors to New Zealand. In 2020, it also returned to Algeria the skulls of those who resisted French colonization in the nineteenth century. This last restitution, hurriedly organized and undertaken out of political calculation rather than sincere contrition, contained twenty-four skulls, though only six were positively identified as belonging to Algerian fighters killed by French colonial troops. It remains the case that France possesses one of the largest collections of human remains in the world, a total of 18,000 relics, according to an audit conducted in 2018. Among them are the remains of the wife of the founder of the Toucouleur Empire in West Africa, those of a Sudanese general, those of an Inuit family exhibited in 1881 in a human zoo. And so many other severed heads of indigenous peoples.[2]

The most noteworthy restitution was the Hottentot Venus,[3] the name given to Sarah Baartman, a Khoikhoi woman from the Eastern Cape region, today part of South Africa. Forced into slavery, she was exhibited in Europe for people to gawp at her steatopygia (large amounts of fat in the buttocks) and elongated labia like an animal at a fair. Destitute, she died in Paris in December 1815, several months after her final exhibition for three long days under the gaze of the scientists of the Museum of Natural History, with its administrator, the naturalist Geoffroy Saint-Hilaire, standing in the front row. Prisoner of the "cruel, ingenious cage" of an anatomic panopticon,[4] to adapt the term of Michel Foucault, she was dissected after her death by the promoter of comparative anatomy George Cuvier, in an autopsy that lasted sixteen hours. The Hottentot Venus was promoted as a symbol of monstrous otherness, specifically associated with Blackness, in order to celebrate, by contrast, a white normality. Her remains were only restored to South Africa in 2002. Previously, for four decades, from 1938 until the 1970s, a life-sized model of her body, fully nude, was exhibited in a window display of the Museum of Humanity in the Palais de Chaillot.

"Here they are ripe, these fruits of a shady destiny." Thus begins "Nocturne," a poem by Saint-John

Perse, who in a parallel life was known as Alexis Leger and served as secretary-general of the French Foreign Office from 1933 through 1940, when Europe was about to be swallowed up by the Nazi night. Part shadow, part light; day and night; garden versus jungle ... In the Jardin des Plantes in Paris, "Nocturne" appears on a bronze sculpture in honor of its poet, who was born in Guadeloupe to a family of white Creoles, which means they were colonists. In a conjunction of opposites, the sculpture is installed not far from the tree planted in memory of Atai, whose severed head was carried back as a trophy of victory over the colonized people.

I could go on forever, for this storehouse of natural wonders under the care of scrupulous gardeners, a place I like so much, is the secret home of a shadowy colonial past that is far from settled. If we make the effort to see and know that history, there are many other places in the French capital where similar— and no less impressive—phantoms prowl. For example, the Élysée Palace, seat of the presidency of the republic and residence of the leader of the state, was built in 1720 with the fortune of Antoine Crozat, whose immense wealth was mainly derived from trading in African slaves. And the construction of the Eiffel Tower, a symbol of France throughout the entire world, was in large part financed by the punitive debt that France imposed upon Haiti in the nineteenth century as the price for having the audacity to revolt and win its independence.

More than all the other former imperial powers, France is deeply affected by the ongoing presence of its colonial past as it negotiates its relationship with the world and fashions its view of itself. Like the violent eruption of something repressed, the vehement persistence of that past was revealed on the far side of the world during the presidency of Emmanuel Macron, when the decolonization accords, signed with New Caledonia in 1988 after French armed forces massacred Kanak independence activists on the island of Ouvéa, were disavowed, reviving an aggressive and conquering colonialism.

Of course, other European nations are still occupied by their imperial past as well, as they work to manage cultural legacies and the question of memory. But it is especially in France that the colonial question remains a live political issue. Simultaneously impassioned and concrete, it determines ongoing ideological debates and governmental priorities. Unpacking this question reveals social issues (the formation and renewal of the working class through the injection of relationships, exchanges, and migrations from elsewhere), democratic issues (the fusion, under the weight of a presidential monarchy, of a single vertical source of power with the sameness of national identity), and international issues (the relationship to diversity, plurality, and fragility of an interdependent world where the universal constructs itself through exchange and sharing, rather than through domination and submission).

This insistence of the colonial question sets France apart from the other historic continental powers that contributed to the projection of Europe upon the world—where, even as the West was building up its wealth through the early accumulation of capital, it was invented politically as judge and model for the other peoples and cultures upon which it imposed itself by force and conquest. French decolonization was simultaneously the latest (with the exception of Portugal, which took place a dozen years after Algeria's independence), the least consensual (the sixteen years from 1945 until 1962 saw uninterrupted colonial wars, from Madagascar to Algeria, by way of Indochina and Cameroon), and the least complete (France is now the sole direct colonial power, with overseas departments and territories, without taking into account its neocolonies, still very much alive, from the Ivory Coast to Chad).

Earlier, at the end of the eighteenth century and over the course of the nineteenth, the British and Spanish empires were forced to surrender sovereignty over certain of their territories (starting with the United States of America and followed by the nations of South America), when slave-holding colonists from those nations demanded independence. The case was entirely different for France. Its colonial jewel, then called Saint-Domingue, was ripped from the metropole in 1804 thanks to a revolt by the oppressed: Haiti was the scene of the fourth of those ancient revolutions, the slave revolution led by the "Black Spartacus," Toussaint Louverture,[5] whose radicalism undermined the three other revolutions—the parliamentarian revolution of Britain, the independence movement of the United States, and the republican revolution in France—and for whose audacity the Haitian people would pay the price—in the literal sense of the word, as mentioned above—in the form of financial compensation until the middle of the twentieth century.

Germany and Italy lost their colonial empires in their European defeats, at the end of World War I for the former, and World War II for the latter. By contrast, after the majority of its political, economic, and intellectual elite had consented to collaborate with the Nazis, France managed to find a seat at the victors' table in 1945, but only because of the mobilization of the colonies, which furnished the bulk of the soldiers of Free France, that improbable army that established the legitimacy of Charles de Gaulle.

Finally, Portugal, the European country that was the first to conquer distant lands, was also, five centuries later, the one for whom decolonization was synonymous with democratization. In 1974, the Carnation Revolution, which brought an end to the dictatorship of António de Oliveira Salazar and instituted democracy, was led by soldiers who had participated in Portugal's "dirty wars" in Africa (Angola, Mozambique, Guinea-Bissau, and Cape Verde). France's final colonial crisis, the Algerian War, moved in the opposite direction by giving birth in 1958 to a military coup against the democratic regime with the hope, ultimately stymied, of maintaining the French empire in North Africa.

That coup was the birth certificate of the Fifth Republic, which lasts to this day, a regime so feebly democratic that it still merits the description by François Mitterrand, in a 1964 essay, as a "permanent coup d'état." It also marked the unequivocal renaissance of the far right, which had been defeated in 1945, and which found its rallying cry in French Algeria. Algeria was also where the future leader of the National Front (later to become the National Rally, under his daughter, Marine), Jean-Marie Le Pen made his debut as a deputy in Pierre Poujade's populist movement and as a torturer.[6]

Published in 2016, a major survey conducted by the National Institute for Demographic Studies (INED) on the diversity of the populations in France established that 14 percent of the French population was born outside the metropole, and that a further 15 percent were the children of those born outside the metropole, be they French, immigrants, or people from the French overseas departments.[7] That means that almost a third of the population is more or less intimately tied to the colonial history of France, not counting all those who, without being French, were impacted by France's projection outside its hexagonal European borders, particularly during the decades of its late and painful decolonization. Furthermore, the INED survey demonstrated that the populations connected to colonial migrations felt particularly invested in the political life of the nation. They demanded civic integration, even while embodying the plurality of identities that makes France a multicultural nation.

Moreover, even now, in the twenty-first century, France is the main colonial power in the world, the sole nation that plants its tricolor flag on all continents with the exception of Asia: from French Guiana to New Caledonia and Polynesia, and from the Antilles to Mayotte and La Réunion. France is thus the last man standing of European colonialism, its overseas possessions representing so many Western outposts in the global "jungle." With 18 percent of its territory found overseas (accounting for 4 percent of its population), France possesses, thanks to these distant lands, the second largest maritime domain after the United States. That colonial presence is an anomaly of history, given that international treaties and conventions since World War II have recognized the right of peoples to self-determination. Paradoxically, this exception also blinds France to its own reality, when it refuses, through colonial prejudice, to recognize its multicultural dimension, the diversity of its origins, and the plurality of its cultures.

Nearly half a century ago, in 1976, *Le Monde* ran a series of long articles on "the empire's confetti" that opened with this question: "Is France the last colonial power of the Western world? This question might startle French people of good faith, for whom, after the independence of Algeria and the countries of Black Africa, the 'colonial file' has long been closed."[8] Since 1962, the French ruling elite, together with their intellectual and media counterparts, had in effect written the colonial question out of public debate entirely. It was as if, with the independence won by numerous colonies, culminating with Algeria in 1962, the question had permanently been put to rest, handed over to peoples who had become sovereign and whose lands no longer counted as France.

So deeply held was this belief that *Realms of Memory*, a famous collection of essays on French history that appeared in multiple volumes between 1984 and 1992,[9] pauses to examine no traces of France's imperialist past, with the exception of the Paris Colonial

Exhibition of 1931. The Black Code of 1685, the long era of slavery, the Haitian revolution, the republic's imperialist conquests, the Algerian War—not one is visible in this monument to a history that is rooted in Europe, defined by immobility and the perpetuity of a "national identity" that excludes the various and distant places that have woven the actual fabric of France's past and present. As Marcel Detienne emphasizes in *L'Identité nationale, une énigme* [National identity: An enigma], this erasure is an attempt to renew the idea of a nation constructed on "sameness" ("to be the same, to remain the same"), an idea whose symbolic violence toward the diversity of France's populations legitimizes and reinforces a very concrete state violence, police violence, in particular.[10]

Fortunately, the publication in 2017 of *France in the World: A New Global History*, edited by Patrick Boucheron, forms a counterweight to this narrative.[11] In this work, we see France's answer to 1492, the year that Christopher Columbus set sail and the Jews were expelled from Spain, which occurred when Louis XIV (on the throne from 1654–1715) got caught up in "[c]rusades against Islam in the Mediterranean, religious purges, conversions and expulsions [of Protestants], colonial ambition, mass enslavement, supremacist ideology."[12] We remember that in 1791, when the revolution of the "Black

Jacobins" began, Saint-Domingue was the beating heart of French colonial trade and the top producer of sugar and coffee in the world, thanks to the fervid exploitation of more than 500,000 slaves, two-thirds of whom were born in Africa and supplied by the vigorous slave trade that generated the substantial wealth of Nantes, Bordeaux, Le Havre, and even Marseille. We unpack Ernest Renan's famous address about the nation, delivered in 1882, just as the French Republic was about to embrace colonialism, and see that its main idea was about how "to make integration into French society difficult for those who come from elsewhere and do not recognize themselves here."[13]

But no historian's riposte is enough to reverse the resolute tendency of a public discourse that is determined to bury, expel, or disallow the colonial question. Instead of disavowing colonialism, we hear about its "positive role" (in a law passed by the National Assembly in 2005 before being repealed by President Jacques Chirac in the following year), the stigmatization of "public contrition" for colonial acts (first appearing during the presidency of Nicolas Sarkozy), the demonization of minority groups for practicing "separatism" (a law passed during the presidency of Emmanuel Macron), an assault upon "decolonial" discourse in the academy (particularly in appeals by intellectuals, including historian Pierre

Nora, a member of the Académie Française), and more. This official French resistance to any expression or mobilization of those impacted by colonialism is the best illustration of what it has attempted to repress.

This is a notable contrast with the United States, where racial segregation has kept the history of slavery present. Starting in the 1960s, it has produced a political and intellectual awareness that has galvanized broad progressive forces aligning themselves with emancipation. Nothing of the sort exists in France, where anti-colonialism has long been confined to the political margins, shouldered by dissidents and minorities, even if their intellectual aura makes them famous abroad, like the Surrealist movement. So it's no surprise if a nationalist sentiment in France—primarily among the right but sometimes even the left—leads to denunciations of a pernicious American influence, epitomized by "wokeism." Derived from the verb to wake, this term is nothing more than a call to wake up and refuse to ignore injustices of any kind. This caricature, with hints of anti-American xenophobia, aims to delegitimize a concrete expression of the common goals of equality found at the intersection of class, race, and gender oppression.

France's long-delayed reckoning comes at the risk of a heavy price, as witnessed by the steady electoral rise of the far right over four decades, which has been accompanied by more and more overt manifestations of racist violence. France is the soil where the deadly new ideology of the "great replacement" first appeared, which is inspiring a neofascist renaissance in Europe and elsewhere in the world, and is even being expressed in acts of terrorism. This theory, invented by Renaud Camus and popularized by Éric Zemmour, both of them French, is a call to obliterate every form of plurality by claiming it to be an existential threat.

The "great replacement" has the same roots as the modern anti-Semitism that was already taking shape in France at the end of the nineteenth century, when the republic made its choice for colonial expansion. At that time, the anti-Semite Édouard Drumont was elected to represent Algiers in the Chamber of Deputies. Drumont, who invented the xenophobic slogan "France for the French," as the motto of his journal, *La Libre parole*, wrote the immensely popular *La France juive* [Jewish France]. The book's fantastical vision of a nation overrun by the Jewish "other" was the first ideological foundation of the European genocide that would be committed by Nazi Germany with the collaboration of Pétain's France and others. Of course, we are not in the same place now. But for as long as it persists, the repression of the colonial issue exposes France—and through France, all of Europe—to ominous reversals and weakens any antidote to the resurgence of racism. From this point of view, although Jacques Chirac made a belated recognition in 1995, during a commemoration of the mass arrests that occurred at the Vélodrome d'Hiver, of the responsibility borne by the French under the Vichy state for the crime against humanity suffered by the Jews of Europe, that recognition remains incomplete. A corresponding acknowledgment regarding the crimes of colonization has yet to be heard.

It is time to look our European history in the face, all of it. Hannah Arendt, when putting together the three parts of *The Origins of Totalitarianism*, makes imperialism the bridge between anti-Semitism and totalitarianism.[14] Nazism was a colonialism of extermination, formed when the imperialist violence previously unleashed upon the continents of colonial conquests made its way back to Europe and began to target populations, cultures, or civilizations that it defined as inferior and nonnative.

Building upon Arendt's premise, Enzo Traverso insists on the "European roots of National Socialism," opposing the tendency, common in France, "to eject the Nazi crimes from the trajectory of the Western world."[15] After explaining that "instances of colonial violence [were] the first implementation of the exterminatory potentialities of modern racist discourse," Traverso adds: "There is no attempt here to blank out the uniqueness of Nazi violence by simply assimilating it to the massacres of colonialism. But we do need to recognize that it was perpetrated in the middle of a war of conquest and extermination waged between 1941 and 1945, which was conceived as a colonial war within Europe." He goes on to insist that "Nazism brought together and fused two paradigmatic figures: the Jew, the 'other' of the Western world, and the subhuman (*Untermensch*), the 'other' of the colonized world."[16]

This colonial blind spot continues to saturate numerous political and intellectual lineages in Europe. As a result, with the exception of marginalized minorities and fleeting bursts of energy, the left in France has never taken a stand against colonialism. In fact, it is the Social Democrats—through the actions of the SFIO, ancestor of the Socialist Party—who bear the responsibility for the colonial wars, which, particularly in Algeria, perpetrated crimes, including widespread torture, as a means to delay independence. None of the politicians in charge have been called to account. So far from it that the chief among them, Robert Lacoste, governor-general and minister of Algeria from February 1956 through May 1958, quietly served as the social deputy in the National Assembly and later as senator until 1980, before dying in 1989 at the age of ninety.

Beyond that shameful case, the creed of French politics, across its diverse spectrum, is predominantly assimilationist, espousing the cult of a republic where a great One (the presidential power) is joined to a great Sameness (the national identity). Neither of France's two major historical pedigrees on the left, the socialists and the communists, has been completely inoculated from this profoundly colonial ideology that demands that "the Other" divest itself of anything specific or distinctive. Even when expressing solidarity with the Other, they betray a certain reluctance for that Other to organize its own affairs by asserting a "fraternalism" that is both condescending and dominating, and which Aimé Césaire denounced when making his break with the Communist Party in his 1956 "Letter to Maurice Thorez."[17] Tensions regarding France's normative secularism repeatedly bubble up, breaking the promise of the liberal law from 1905 that grants minorities the freedom to exercise their religion, while racist individuals recite polemics about "non-mixed" gatherings. Such events illustrate an oppressive assimilationist tendency, of which the Muslim part of the French population bears the cost today, when they are urged to be less Muslim in order to become more French.

Moreover, the active rejection of the colonial issue, the refusal to address and resolve it, which strengthens the cause of the far right, has been carried out by a network drawn from the ranks of the left under the name Printemps républicain [Republican spring]. Their ideology is a return to the essay mentioned above by Ernest Renan, the official thinker of the republican order, who in 1882 asked, "What is a nation?" And the answer? "A soul, a spiritual principle, a referendum held daily."

Yet only a decade earlier, this same Renan wrote the following in *Intellectual and Moral Reform*: "Colonization on a large scale is an absolutely first-order political necessity. A nation that does not colonize is irrevocably destined to socialism, to the war of the rich against the poor. The conquest of a country of an inferior race by a superior race, which settles there to govern it, has nothing shocking to it...In the same way that conquests between equal races are reprehensible, the regeneration of inferior or mongrel races by superior races fits within the providential order of humanity."[18]

This idea and these words, which today are considered far right, were at that time considered representative of political thought in the French Republic. It is not enough, therefore, to rally around the idea of "the republic"—a republic without qualification, a republic that is neither democratic nor social, a republic that ignores its faults and its past crimes—as though the fact or the name of a republic guarantees a hopeful future. Still less to suggest that France stands apart as a universal exception and leads the way when meeting other nations of the world, with their needs and challenges. Far from it! Doing so only guarantees impotence and deadlock.

So long as France—and Europe as well—has not resolved the colonial question, it will remain at the mercy of its historic ideologies of inequality (regarding races, peoples, cultures, civilizations, and so on), and by consequence, the political ruins it has birthed (imperialism, racism, anti-Semitism, and so on). The political ascension of the far right in France since the start of the 1980s—the very decade when the crisis in New Caledonia came to a head—together with a public discourse that is steadily being conquered by the far right's identitarian refrains—which corrupt public, political, and media spaces—are rooted in this deferral, in which France's unresolved past goes on strangling the present and paralyzing the future.

If we needed tangible proof, the violent crisis in New Caledonia, provoked by France's colonial obstinacy, offers a warning that cannot be written off. On July 14, 2024, when French National Day is celebrated, the anti-independence president of the Assembly for New Caledonia's South Province, Sonia Backès, formerly state secretary for citizenship under the presidency of Emmanuel Macron, unambiguously called for a renewal of apartheid, which is to say, separation on the grounds of origin, culture, appearance, or racial identity—everything that racists define as race. "To the same degree that oil and water do not mix," she declared, "I regretfully state that the Kanak world and the Western world, despite 170 years of shared life, have antagonisms that remain unsurmountable." Referring to differences found in "political systems, feudal for the one and democratic for the other," and in "relationships to the economy, communal for the one and capitalistic for the other," she distinguishes "two civilizations," clearly asserting the superiority of one over the other. She concludes by proposing the separation of the South Province, where Europeans form the primary demographic group, from the North Province, where the Kanak population forms the majority. "When two forces oppose each other, and two camps are convinced of the legitimate defense of their values, they find themselves faced with a choice: a battle to the death of one of the two, or else separation for a better life," declares this spokesperson of a colonialism still dynamic and pernicious.

No people will be free so long as it oppresses another: this statement, a familiar refrain from all decolonizing fights, remains valid. It is in this sense that the future of Europe is playing out in Oceania, in New Caledonia, through the politics of French colonialism. Either France persists in its logic of appropriation, power, and domination, at the risk of carrying back to the heart of its continental hexagon those authoritarian, identitarian, and racist politics, or else it seizes this opportunity to liberate itself from the colonial issue by granting the full independence of a unified New Caledonia, as sought by the activists of Kanaky. In doing so, France would usher in a renaissance that elevates it above the democratic and social breakdowns that today are wounding and diminishing it.

Europe will not neutralize its current identitarian and authoritarian threats unless it faces up to the colonial past that has shaped it for so long and liberates itself from the colonial present that France is actively carrying on. No country has been colonized with impunity, asserts Aimé Césaire in his *Discourse on Colonialism*, which is essential to reread for the lifeline it offers in the face of contemporary regressions. "Colonization: bridgehead in a campaign to civilize barbarism, from which there may emerge the negation of civilization, pure and simple."[19] Still afire with force and beauty, this text speaks directly to a France that is digging in its heels to refuse the right of peoples for self-determination. It proclaims that the Nazi barbarity that ravaged Europe drew its starting point, its fury, and its energy from colonial violence.

From this point of view, Césaire is saying the same thing as Hannah Arendt, who saw imperialism as the moment when the scales tipped toward totalitarianism. And it is precisely here where the unresolved crux of the European debate lies: there is no Hitler without colonialism, no European catastrophe without colonial savagery, no Nazism without racism, and no genocide without the ideology of superior civilizations and races. Césaire, never one to mince words, censures "the very distinguished, very humanistic, very Christian bourgeois of the twentieth century" in the following way: "what he cannot forgive Hitler for is not *the crime* in itself, *the crime against man*, it is not *the humiliation of man as such*, it is the crime against the white man, the humiliation of the white man, and the fact that he applied to Europe colonialist procedures which until then had been reserved exclusively for the Arabs of Algeria, the 'coolies' of India, and the 'niggers' of Africa."[20]

This great poet makes the political connection and drives home the point: "And that is the great thing I hold against pseudo-humanism: that for too long it has diminished the rights of man, that its concept of those rights has been—and still is—narrow and fragmentary, incomplete and biased and, all things considered, sordidly racist... At the end of capitalism, which is eager to outlive its day, there is Hitler. At the end of formal humanism and philosophic renunciation, there is Hitler."[21]

Césaire saw right, and he spoke the truth: Hitler is not extraneous to us. The political monstrosity that came to life upon our continent is the fruit of European crimes committed against others. In order to speak to the world, Europe, whose peoples are woven from the diverse threads tied to the colonial histories of their countries, must make this painful truth our shared political awareness. Yes, no one can colonize with impunity, and France knows better than anyone the terrible price to be paid for this crime, from the invention of modern anti-Semitism (in the Dreyfus affair) to the widespread use of state torture (in the Algerian War).

The Dreyfus affair, in which modern anti-Semitism was built upon the foundation of an old Christian anti-Judaism, began in 1894 and divided France between the Dreyfusards, who supported Alfred Dreyfus, a Jewish officer in the French military, and the Anti-Dreyfusards, who unjustly accused him of treason. Less than ten years had passed from the colonial turning point of the Third Republic in 1885, when a decision to pursue the conquest of Madagascar and Indochina saw the republic embrace a colonial empire that was initially launched by the Bourbon Restoration (the conquest of Algeria began shortly before the July Revolution of 1830) and expanded in the 1850s and 1860s by the Second French Empire (Mayotte, Tahiti, the Marquesas, New Caledonia, Senegal, southern Vietnam, and Cambodia).

The new colonial charge was led by Jules Ferry, the prime minister whose name is associated in France with free, compulsory public school education. "It must be said clearly: yes, superior races have a right with respect to inferior races...I repeat that superior races have a right, because they also have a duty, and that is to civilize the inferior races." This same Ferry, who would earn the taunting moniker of Ferry-Tonkin after the Tonkin Affair in 1885, would go so far as to say that the 1789 Declaration of the Rights of Man "was not written for the Blacks of equatorial Africa."

The Anti-Dreyfusards were also colonialists to the extreme. They were the intellectual avant-garde of the colonial poison that was spreading through Europe: the inferiorization of man to the point of negation. This inferiorization, tied inextricably to the abomination of colonialism, provides the origin of the genocide of Europe's Jews. We see it in the bestial imagination that accompanied the crime, for example in the anti-Semitic philippic by Robert Brasillach, a future collaborator with the Nazis, published in the March 31, 1939, edition of the newspaper *Je suis partout*: "What tribunal would dare condemn us, if we denounced the extraordinary invasion of Paris and France by monkeys?...You go to the theater? The hall is filled with monkeys...On the bus? In the subway? Monkeys...In the countryside, in the markets, at the fairs, whole stands are occupied by monkeys, offering discount prices on a heap of pans and fabrics taken from bankruptcies... The females by their side, decked out in furs and strings of pearls, simper in a manner almost human... That which we call anti-simianism (read the word well, I beg!) becomes, each day, an ever more pressing need..."

Or take the example of the "negroid Jew" in the anti-Semitic pamphlets by the writer Louis-Ferdinand Céline. The racist colonial imagination of the *nègres* nourished the exterminating frenzy toward the Jews, who, for the anti-Semite, are non-whites. At the very beginning of his *Discourse on Colonialism*, Aimé Césaire also says this: "A civilization that uses its principles for trickery and deceit is a dying civilization. The fact is that the so-called European civilization—'Western' civilization—as it has been shaped by two centuries of bourgeois rule, is incapable of solving the two major problems to which its existence has given rise: the problem of the proletariat and the colonial problem..."[22]

These words, though dated by their circumstances (Césaire was a member of the Communist Party while serving as Martinque's deputy to the National Assembly of France), remain relevant today. Especially in France, that "America of Europe" by virtue of its diverse population, where the social question and the colonial question are permanently intertwined. Not to confront the latter is to doom the former. That is exactly what has been confirmed for us in these past decades by the spectacle of leaders being pulled in various directions by identitarian tensions, when they turn away from social demands to the same degree that they equivocate regarding the urgent need for truth about the colonial question, past and present.

It would be sufficient, however, to listen to voices that, refusing to be consigned to servitude, have shown the way, the path of a true humanism, showing respect for equal human beings and for equal civilizations, in all their plurality and their differences. Thus, Frantz Fanon tells us at the end of *Black Skin, White Masks*: "I, a man of color, want but one thing: May man never be instrumentalized. May the subjugation of man by man—that is to say, of me by another—cease. May I be allowed to discover and desire man, wherever he may be. The black man is not. No more than the white man... Superiority? Inferiority? Why not simply try to touch the other, feel the other, discover each other? Was my freedom not given to me to build the world of *you*?"[23]

It's this "world of *you*" that Louise Michel, deported to New Caledonia in 1873 for her role in the Paris Commune, endeavors to build when she makes her way toward the Kanak people, discovering their culture, deciphering their language, listening to their legends.[24] It was a solitary path at a time when unrestrained colonial violence raged, barefaced, in all its ugliness. We can only turn this colonial page if we read this history to the end—and we won't emerge from this reading unscathed.

See what a naval commander writes in the 1870s to Admiral Martin Fourichon, then minister of the colonies: "The Caledonian is intelligent but a monster of perversity. We must begin by destroying this population if we want to live in peace in this country. The only way that seems somewhat practical for getting rid of them is to hunt them down, as we do wolves in France, with several detachments of thirty men, and destroy the plantations, the villages, launching new raids several times per day when it's about to rain."

But see also other deported members of the Paris Commune, who, when confronted by Atai's revolt in 1878, called for a pitiless repression against "the brutalities of peoples a little too primitive." In this way, they deny the Kanak, who were simply defending their own land, the same right to rise up that they claimed for themselves in Paris. One of them did not hesitate to write, "In order to bring security to colonization, it is necessary that the majority of these people disappear," while another affirms that he only sees "safety for the colony through mass extermination."

Colonialism is a pitiless gauge, putting the truth of humanism and the reality of equality to the test. "Enough of this superiority, which only reveals itself through destruction!" cries Louise Michel, on the contrary, in her memoirs, when she looks back on her forced exile in New Caledonia. On the eve of Atai's insurrection in 1878, two Kanaks from the Isle of Pines came to pay her a visit and bid her "farewell before going off to swim through the storm to rejoin their people and beat the wicked whites, they said." In that moment, Michel recounts, "I took the red scarf of the Commune that I had preserved through a thousand difficulties. I divided it in two to give it to them as a memento."[25]

The fight for equality has no borders. There is no symphony more majestic. Only by approaching the Other, the stranger, the distant, the different can we discover ourselves. For that is also the way of truth, the truth we learn by thinking against ourselves, accepting doubt, and searching for the infinite. By refusing any claim to know in advance, by clearing away false certainties, by discovering that we always have more to learn. Finally, by understanding that no nation, no people, no culture, no civilization is the sole possessor of the universal, nor the sole heir of the right, still less the seat of humanism.

On June 26, 1875, three years before Atai's great revolt broke out, Louise Michel stood before the

Pacific Ocean and wrote these bracing words, inspired by Kanaky:

> *Night falls on the silent bay, and in the shadow the*
> *shoals are barking.*
> *O sea! Before you the spirit calms. To suffer is no*
> *longer enough, to know is all.*
> *But will we ever know? Science is a torch in the*
> *hands of scouts: the farther it is carried forward,*
> *the larger the shadow grows behind.*
> *Which chasm shall we sound to search out the truth?*
> *Is there a utopia that does not become reality when*
> *its time comes? It there a science that must not*
> *be transformed? No matter! On we search, the*
> *horizon brightens.*
> *As we wait, let us tell old Europe the stories of*
> *humanity's childhood.*

6 ▸ A VILLA IN THE JUNGLE

"A VILLA IN THE JUNGLE." Many prominent figures in Israel do not hesitate to adopt such terms when describing their country within the region of the world where it has existed since 1948.

Without a doubt, that year stands out as a landmark, highlighting all that has been at risk ever since. It was on May 14, 1948, that David Ben-Gurion proclaimed the creation of the State of Israel, in the wake of the plan adopted by the United Nations on November 29, 1947, to divide Palestine between a Jewish state and an Arab one, though the latter never saw the light of day. In a rare moment of harmony between the United States and the Soviet Union, which were both conscious of the incommensurable crime that had been committed in the destruction of the Jews of Europe, the victories won by the Nazis vindicated the demand of the Zionist movement for a nation-state, based on the Jewish national home existing in Palestine.

Seven months later in Paris, on December 10, 1948, the United Nations ratified the Universal Declaration of Human Rights, which, in its preamble, declared "the rule of law" to be "essential, if man is not to be compelled to have recourse, as a last resort, to rebellion against tyranny and oppression." This provision, which condones resistance against injustice, sums up the terrible contradiction that was immediately bequeathed to the world in the Nakba, the disaster suffered by the Palestinian people when the majority of the Arab population of Palestine was forcibly expelled. By recognizing the State of Israel, Europe and the West repaired the crime committed against the Jewish people in their own continent, yet in doing so, they laid the burden upon the backs of another people, the Palestinians. Since then, indifference, the same trait which permitted the genocide, has lived on, this time with other victims.

Conversing in 2011 with Stéphane Hessel (1917–2013), a UN diplomat who was present at the creation of the Jewish state in Palestine, the French-Palestinian writer Elias Sanbar recalled the origin of this conflict, one that will continue to worsen until it is confronted: "Of course, we cannot rewrite history, but it is important to say that this conflict began with a terrible injustice committed in Palestine as a way to repair another injustice, born in the horror of the Nazi camps."[1] A participant in the Israeli-Palestinian peace negotiations, Sanbar was convinced that the only solution would be found in equal rights. Reciprocity and recognition. The inverse of the poison that is a competition in victimhood. The opposite of the misery that is the victor's goodwill.

"It must be said," Sanbar went on, "that a competition in the catalog of misfortunes is indecent, that a race to the highest number of dead is literally obscene. Each suffering is unique: the fact that the Jews were exterminated does nothing to ease the suffering of the Palestinians, just as the fact that the Palestinians have suffered and continue to suffer does nothing to ease the horror lived by the Jews. Above all, recognizing the suffering of others never delegitimizes your own suffering. On the contrary."

You cannot erase a crime with an injustice. If you do, it will come back to haunt you. That is where we are, unfortunately, ever since Israel, which was born as compensation for a genocide, was in its turn accused of committing one, in response to the massacres on October 7, 2023.

This fatal cycle brings us back to the Israeli metaphor of the villa in the jungle. Like a well-worn maxim, this image of a peaceable domicile surrounded by a hostile nature has been taken up by journalists, intellectuals, and politicians. "Israel: 'A

Villa in the Jungle'" is the title of an article in *Le Débat* under the byline of the historian Ran Halévi, who began his education at the Hebrew University of Jerusalem.[2] The renowned Israeli journalist and war veteran Ron Ben-Yishaï uses the same terms: "For us, Israel is 'a villa in the jungle.' We want to protect our villa, but also to make the jungle a less hostile place."[3] But it is an Israeli military leader and politician who most notably promoted the formula: Ehud Barak, whose career progressed from commander-in-chief of the IDF, minister of foreign affairs, prime minister, and most important, defense minister.

It was in this final role, when he was preparing to launch one of the numerous Israeli wars against Gaza—Operation Cast Lead, in 2008, which lasted twenty-two days—that Barak developed at length this image of a country surrounded by the jungle. Significantly, an interview with him, appearing in the journal *Les Temps modernes*, is titled "L'Ombre et la lumière" [The shadow and the light],[4] and if we could preserve only one piece of evidence to measure the perverse mechanism of every colonialism, this could be that document. The man who speaks is not a religious fundamentalist, fanatical and supremacist; his convictions lie a thousand miles from the racism displayed by the extreme Israeli right that came to power with Benjamin Netanyahu; and the Labor Party, whose colors he wears, was a member of Socialist International before joining the Progressive Alliance. However, Barak adopts here the same vision of the world closing in like a radical Other. No lasting compromise is possible, and there is no imaginable coexistence apart from perpetual war. Anticipating the war triggered against Gaza in 2023 after the terrorist massacres by Hamas, we even find this self-assurance: "We do not wish to launch a large-scale invasion in the Gaza Strip, but we probably have no alternative. We will not be diverted from it, even in the face of a negative judgment from the rest of the world."

But the main point lies elsewhere, in the vision of the Other: the Palestinian, with whom Israel cohabitates, and the East, where its nation-state was born in 1948. What is it that Barak says? That Israel will never be accepted by its neighbors, that the world surrounding it will never be its own, and that as a result, it will forever be necessary to make war in order to assert itself and survive. For as Barak says, "we are conscious of living in the jungle."

Take the time to judge for yourself:

The view that Israelis have of themselves can be compared to that of the peoples of Western Europe and North America. They want normality and are ready to pay the necessary price. But on the other hand, we are not ready to be victims of the circumstances imposed by our neighborhood... The good news is that Israel was, is, and will be, for the foreseeable future, the strongest country within a radius of 1,500 kilometers [930 miles] of Jerusalem... We are by far the strongest, militarily and strategically. And we are conscious of living in the jungle. It's a difficult neighborhood. Nothing at all like Western Europe or North America. It's a neighborhood with no pity for the weak, and no second chances for those who do not know how to defend themselves. If you do not defend yourself, you disappear. We know that, and we are ready to fight... Today, people understand more and more how hard this region is. As I say, the Middle East is not the Midwest. So we have to stand strong on our own two feet, eyes wide open, ready to extend a hand, the left hand, if possible, to open all the doors, all the windows in a search of opportunities for making peace. But eyes wide open, looking reality full in the face. And with the other hand, the right hand, if possible, the finger is on the trigger to be able to shoot. At point-blank range, ready to shoot if necessary to defend our survival. I believe it's very clear at the current moment... that we must find a way to live with this reality, to know that the people around us do not love us. Many of them dream that we might disappear and go back to where we came from.

The frankness of these remarks justifies the length of the citation. We find a distillation of colonial thought in the mouth of Ehud Barak, this representative not of the far right, but of Israel's equivalent to the Socialist Party: indigenous people are fundamentally threatening and dangerous; colonialists are a foreign body in the region that receives them; violence defines the relationship between the two populations; colonization embodies a tiny island of civilization confronting the jungle that encircles it; while the colonized is trapped in an essentialized identity, the colonizer claims to be on the side of the universal. Not only is this an ideological vision of reality that can lead to lethal dead ends, as we know from Europe's experience, it is even more an unrealistic vision, and therefore irresponsible, just as it has been from the first moment it was expressed.

Because what Ehud Barak is proposing is an Israel engaged in ceaseless war, perpetually subduing its neighborhood by force, living in fear and worry, its survival guaranteed only by military power that is not necessarily eternal, dependent as it is upon the support of the United States. Paradoxically, the state that, on the day after the genocide, symbolized the hope that Jews could finally live in security, has thus become the place where they will be in greatest peril, threatened and attacked. That is what the attack by

Hamas on October 7, 2023, made concrete, creating an existential panic in the heart of the Israeli population.

Even if, by the sole power of its military might, the State of Israel survives in this way, nothing will remain of its democratic appearance or its internal diversity. It will no longer be anything but a "state run by rabbis and generals,"[5] as prophesized in 2007 by Avraham Burg, former speaker of the Knesset (the Israeli parliament) and chairman of the World Zionist Organization, in a poignant book, in which he does not hesitate to affirm that the Israeli Arabs are like the German Jews of the Second Reich.[6] Burg's insight echoes another prophecy, enunciated the day after the conquests and occupations of 1967 by Yeshayahu Leibowitz: "We are condemned to live in our country without peace and security." This scholar, who was editor in chief of the *Encyclopedia Hebraica*, added that from that time onward, "The corruption characteristic of every colonial regime would also prevail in the state of Israel," and that all the preoccupations of the state and of the government "would be concerned only with the specific problems... of ruling over both Jews and Arabs."[7]

Indeed, in the same interview with *Les Temps modernes*, Ehud Barak worries that Israel has "too many different groups," saying that it is necessary to "watch out for strife." Barak evokes the specter of a "civil war" in Israel and concludes by potentially excluding from the Israeli population the Arabs who are still citizens there: "There are three powerful, centrifugal forces working against us: we have an important population, 20 percent, that are non-Jews, primarily Arabs, and some of them feel empathy for, or identify with, the Palestinian people."

What a terrible admission of failure! Especially when this confession comes from a figure who symbolizes Israeli military power and the political tradition, the Labor Party, that dominated Israel's first three decades. And so the Zionist utopia where the Jews of the entire world could finally feel themselves secure is here defined as the most hostile and threatening environment, with no future beyond permanent war against the world that surrounds it. And with no strategy other than to drag the whole Western world into this madness of war, murder, and devastation. Lost in blindness toward itself and indifference to the fate of others, every colonial adventure ends in ruin for the people who deem themselves its beneficiary.

As long as Israel's leaders do not confront head-on the original injustice committed against the Palestinians, as long as they persist in prolonging and increasing their occupation and colonialization of the Palestinian territories (notably in violation of the resolutions adopted by the United Nations after the annexations of 1967), as long as they insist upon denying to the Palestinian people the right to live in a sovereign state (in violation of the Oslo Accords of 1993), history will stall and move backward. As demonstrated by the unprecedented martyrdom suffered by the Palestinian people in the hour I write these lines, there is great risk of an unlimited retrogression. If any proof were needed, Israel's allies need only look at the vote by the Knesset taken in the middle of war on July 18, 2024, to reject categorically the creation of a Palestinian state, defined as an "existential danger for the State of Israel and its citizens." It was a vote meant to snub the Western powers and their habitual diplomatic litanies about the "two-state solution."

Since then, not only is a part of our humanity dying in Gaza, with tens of thousands of massacred civilians, our entire soul is also being lost, through indifference to their fate. The soul of Israel will no longer survive, despite all its military boasting. Blind power is unlimited weakness. If it makes no effort to examine and question itself, the State of Israel, a colonizer with no other homeland, is condemned to destroy the democratic ideals that it claims for its own citizens while denying them to the Palestinians. If it manages to survive, it will end up barricaded behind the illusory walls of an apartheid, which, through separation and expulsion, attempts to erase the presence of the Other so as to banish the fear that is fed by an awareness of the evil it has inflicted. In doing so, Israel puts itself at risk, delegitimizing itself in the eyes of the world through the crimes it commits and accepts, even as it drags its allies along with it and forces them to take part in an identitarian war that brandishes civilization to justify its savagery.

More alarming still, were that even possible, Barak's exceptional confession suggests that this regressive fantasy of unity exists on a world scale, ignoring every difference and dissonance. "We are an outpost of the free world in the middle of this region," Barak asserts, expressing himself like certain French leaders during the Algerian War. Or like Kurtz in Joseph Conrad's novel, who sees himself surrounded by "all the brutes," with no way out except to exterminate them.

"We are on the front lines," insists Barak, pointing to "a triangle of dangers," composed of radical Islamism, nuclear proliferation, and rogue states. "The problem extends across the entire globe," he claims. "Your borders as well are porous. Certain Muslims are going to gain in power and demand a better expression of their rights, and Europe will have to confront that. It's the end of Europe, perceived as an island paradise. You are going to be confronted with the same questions. That has already happened in

Kosovo, in the Netherlands, in the South of France, in England. And I believe that deep down, you know it." Whenever someone vaguely hints at threats rather than intelligently interrogating their causes, we recognize all the explosive ingredients of the "war on terror," declared by the U.S. administration under the presidency of George W. Bush, who read the world through the prism of a clash of civilizations.

Preceded by shameful falsehoods and accompanied by an infinity of human rights violations, including official sanction for torture, the United States' response to September 11 only increased international dangers, ravaged sovereign states, inspired new forms of terrorism, humiliated entire peoples, and unified their lasting resentment. All to the maximal benefit of China and Russia. China rose to the rank of the second—and potentially the first—economic power in the world, while Russia has revived an aggressive imperial logic, from Syria to Ukraine, to say nothing of the African continent. The intervention of the United States, which drapes itself in the very democratic ideals it tramples, has done nothing to support the peoples who are striving to win liberty and democracy. Quite the opposite! The results can be seen after the pitiable retreat of the American military from Afghanistan, where the Taliban returned to power in 2021, notably to the despair of Afghan women.

Turning our gaze elsewhere, a chief target of U.S. aspirations to reorganize the region, the Islamic Republic of Iran, has kept expanding its geopolitical influence, from Iraq to Syria, from Lebanon to Yemen, without forgetting Hamas in Gaza, even as the ruling theocracy represses the hopes of the Iranian people for freedom. For its part, Saudi Arabia, the religious monarchy that was the ideological birthplace of Al-Qaeda, is not at all concerned about its violations of human rights. On the contrary, it imagines itself more than ever to be the center of the world, and it has even been chosen to host a world's fair, Expo 2030. Meanwhile, in Israel, the racist and supremacist far right has solidified its grip on power alongside Benjamin Netanyahu and his allies. That is to say the very same people who ideologically put the gun into the hand of the Jewish terrorist who assassinated Yitzhak Rabin, the Israeli prime minister and former general, during a peace demonstration in Tel Aviv on November 4, 1995, one year after he received the Nobel Peace Prize alongside the Palestinian leader Yasser Arafat.

This radicalization of Israeli politics confirms that every colonialism is a step toward barbarity. As the Israeli-Palestinian conflict demonstrates, the persistence of the colonial question makes the world savage. In a sinister paradox, the historical source of the global catastrophe, colonialism, has continued into the present as reparations for Europe's crime, and has produced the injustice committed against the Palestinians. Colonialism does not civilize; it does the reverse. The resentment generated by the humiliation of dispossessed populations is met with a hardening of the colonial position. The process is both terrifying and unstoppable. It offers a playing field ideally suited to force the community to become a tribe, religion an absolute, and origin a privilege. From there, to accept the colonial fact is to fan the flames of a war of civilizations, seen in the parallel radicalization of the opposing camps: the racist Jewish supremacy of the extreme Israeli right echoes the Islamic ideology of Hamas and its allies, all of which negates the diversity of the Palestinian society.

From a vantage point of two decades, the Israeli reaction to the attack of October 7, 2023, is not only a simple repetition of America's blindness after the assault on September 11, 2001. It's even worse. It risks leading the entire world astray through its ideological excess. The political power that governs Israel today and is in charge of this war embodies a radical rupture by carrying to the farthest extreme the infernal identitarian logic of colonization, the superiority of civilizations, and hierarchy among humans.

Under Benjamin Netanyahu, who has been in power since 2009, with only a brief interruption in

2021–22, Israel has suffered an "identitarian coup" that has advanced the ideology of religious nationalism, as the journalist Charles Enderlin has written.[8] Since 2018, a Basic Law, which is the highest rank of law because this state lacks a constitution, has defined Israel as the "national home of the Jewish people," with no reference to the democratic principle of equal rights.

By legitimizing an identitarian supremacy that discriminates against the Arab and Druze minorities, this law contradicts the Israeli Declaration of Independence of 1948, which directs Israel to ensure "a complete equality of social and political rights for all its citizens, without distinction of belief, race, or sex." No minor demagogic stumble, this ideological radicalization heralds the rise to power in Israel of political forces that embrace a rupture with every universalist vision: no natural equality, no international law, no shared humanity.

Even worse, this ideology is destined to be exported, as demonstrated by the renown that its theorist and propagandist, the Israeli-American Yoram Hazony, enjoys among the far right in the United States and Europe.[9] Hazony's bestselling book *The Virtue of Nationalism*, which has been translated into a score of languages, is nothing more than a contemporary recycling of the full-throated nationalism of Charles Maurras, minus the anti-Semitism, and contains a preface to written by a French propagandist of the far right, Gilles-William Goldnadel.[10]

Denouncing the "fanaticism of the universal" and "liberal imperialism," Hazony's defense of a new governing "order of national states" seeks to end the values promoted by the Universal Declaration of Human Rights in 1948, at the conclusion of World War II, which emphasized how nation-states could become the worst enemies of the human race. Hazony's radical nationalism implies that nations need take only themselves into account and must never cede their power to international institutions: "We should not let a hairbreadth of our freedom be given over to foreign bodies under any name whatsoever," writes Hazony, "or to foreign systems of law that are not determined by our own nation."[11] This rejection of every universal principle is accompanied by an ethnic understanding of the state, which demands the "overwhelming dominance of a single, cohesive nationality" when confronted with tribal or national minorities within its borders.[12]

In this way, the page that was opened in 1948 to a common humanity, guided by universal principles that limit nation-states, was closed once again. It is nothing less than going back to the roots of the catastrophe that began in Europe and was carried around the world, those egotistical nationalisms, so oppressive and dominating, which led to ravages and crimes in the first half of the twentieth century, including genocide, and which in their extreme form produced fascism and Nazism.

When the new war in Gaza began, the Institute of the Arab World in Paris held an exhibit entitled "What Palestine Brings to the World." In the introduction to the exhibit catalog, the journalist Christophe Ayad comments, "Palestine tells of the world as it goes bad...People observe Palestine, scrutinize it, encourage it, or lecture it, but it is Palestine that watches us from the future of our humanity. Palestine already lives in a world that is alienated, surveilled, caged, reduced to savagery, neoliberalized. Palestinians know what it is to be an exile in their own land. Let us learn from them!"[13]

The Palestinians have already taught us that the creed of power is a dead end, while the awareness of fragility, on the contrary, is a force. "Think of Others" is the title and the refrain of a famous poem by Mahmoud Darwish, without a doubt the greatest Arab poet of our modern era and the bard of the Palestinian cause, though his work cannot be reduced to it. "As you conduct your wars, think of others (do not forget those who seek peace),"[14] says his second stanza. This poem is also a witness, for Darwish grew up in the awareness of this care for the Other, even for the enemy. He lived in Israel until 1970, learned

Hebrew as his first foreign language, and discovered European literature in that language.

Think of others. Don't lock yourself away in one closed identity. Don't let passion destroy empathy. Don't savage others at the risk of savaging your soul. Don't abandon this basic sensibility that articulates our concern for the world and the living.

In 1967, when at the conclusion of the Six-Day War, Israel decided to occupy the Palestinian territories, twelve Israeli citizens made the choice to think of others. Published in the *Haaretz* newspaper on September 22, 1967, their appeal was taken up once again on December 28, 2023, by filmmakers from the entire world in order to demand an immediate ceasefire in Gaza.[15]

Here is what they said:

> Our right to defend ourselves from extermination does not give us the right to oppress others.
>
> Occupation entails foreign rule.
>
> Foreign rule entails resistance.
>
> Resistance entails repression.
>
> Repression entails terror and counter-terror.
>
> The victims of terror are mostly innocent people.
>
> Holding on to the occupied territories will turn us into a nation of murderers and murder victims.
>
> Let us get out of the occupied territories immediately.[16]

Its first signatories were present at the birth, in 1962, of an Israeli party that was socialist, internationalist, and anti-colonialist. Its Hebrew name, Matzpen, means "the compass": the compass of equality.

7 ▸ THE CREOLE GARDENS

IN CALAIS, THAT FRENCH city that faces Great Britain across the English Channel, there is a place called the Heath. But when men, women, and children from every corner of the world came and settled there in the hope of making the crossing to England, it received a new name: the Jungle. It was not called the Jungle by the new arrivals, but by the authorities, who sent in the police to persecute, brutalize, and chase them out.

The "jungle" of Calais tells the story of the dehumanization of Europe by refusing to others the right that, for centuries, Europe has never ceased claiming for itself: the right to project itself upon the world, to choose it and to want it, to discover it and to survey it. In its basic meaning, and despite its pitfalls, everything evoked by the word civilization—acts of solidarity and sharing, caretaking and kindness—belongs to these migrants, in their quest for hope and refuge, their heroic journeys across the horizon. Meanwhile, on the contrary, the word de-civilization applies to the powers that pursue them, that destroy their makeshift shelters, deprive them of basic necessities, and make life literally impossible for them. That experience was captured in *The Wild Frontier*, a 2017 documentary film by Nicolas Klotz and Élisabeth Perceval about the "jungle" of Calais, which documents the human dignity of its residents in the face of the dehumanization that they are sub-jected to.

Contrary to what we constantly hear in the offi-cial speeches of politicians, Europe is not experienc-ing a migration crisis but a crisis of welcoming. The migratory apocalypse is a fantastical tale, the inanity of which is constantly demonstrated by the demog-raphers and statisticians of all the international ref-erence bodies, including Eurostat in the European Commission. It is nothing but a double denial of reality, just as François Héran, chair of Migrations and Societies at the Collège de France reminds us: a denial of history, since France is a land of immi-grants, and a denial of sociology, given the perpe-tuity of human migrations.[1] Yet this reminder was powerless to stop the inevitable: the adoption in late 2023, following an initiative by President Emmanuel Macron, who was elected to stop the far right, of the umpteenth anti-immigration law, in accordance with Macron's guiding obsession for "national preference," the idea that government programs prioritize French citizens. Making immigration a threat and exaggerating its scope has no other aim than to impose an ideological shift that destroys the principle of equality. The fate of migrants and exiles, of asylum-seekers and refugees, together with the normalization of policies of erasure of these human beings coming from around the world, becomes a lever that opens a door to the most violent and extreme forms of a resurgent fascism.

The question of hospitality, of providing refuge and asylum, is thus the question of Europe's destiny. As the Mediterranean Sea becomes an enormous maritime cemetery, there are today private initiatives, arising from civil society, which strive to save from drowning these men, women, and children, who with the energy that comes from despair, are simply seeking to live—to live better, live elsewhere, live otherwise, live peaceably. Mare Nostrum [Our sea] was a short-lived operation launched by the Italian Navy, created in light of the shock of a shipwreck, on October 3, 2013, off the large Sicilian island of Lampedusa, of a vessel carrying some 500 African migrants. It was followed soon after, on October 11, 2013, by the loss of a second boat that departed from Libya with 480

passengers, primarily Syrian refugees, and sank between Malta and Lampedusa. The first shipwreck
tallied 366 deaths, while the second was reckoned
at 268, sixty of whom were children.

On the other side, the European Union barri-
cades itself behind a repressive wall as expensive as
it is barbaric, habituating us to the worst. Frontex
(a named derived from *frontières extérieurs*, "external
borders") is the European Border Patrol and Coast
Guard Agency that is designed to reject and repulse.
Its French director from 2015 to 2022 has become a
European deputy of the far right, after having had to
resign in light of an inquest by the European Anti-
Fraud Office. Meanwhile, the financial resources
of Frontex have exploded. From 19 million euros
in 2006, its budget rose to more than 845 million
euros in 2023, already not far from the average annual budget of 900 million euros that is planned by
the European Union for the year 2027. The target for
that year is a force of 10,000 permanent European
border guards. With a total of 6.4 billion euros al-
located for the period 2021–27, Frontex is the most
richly supported of all the agencies of Europe.

Migrants then, and not the climate crisis or social
needs. Clearly, the essential priorities of this Europe
do not count the essential as a priority. It is in this
kind of blindness, where unawareness mixes with
irresponsibility, that the European garden—where

"everything works," in the phrase of Josep Borrell—
becomes our own jungle.

There is "no life without movement," as the Natural History Museum in Paris is keen to remind us
in a manifesto about migrations. "Mobility is indis-
pensable for preserving life on earth," the scholars
behind the piece calmly affirm, recalling the meager
number of migrants "compared to the sum total of
human movements."[2] Confirming that we are not
living through a "migratory crisis," but instead a crisis of welcoming, they emphasize that "encounter"
is the beating heart of life: "If we view things on the
broad scale of time, intermixing promotes the adap-
tive potential of populations, be they vegetable, animal, or human." Then, citing Kant and his project
of universal peace, they finish by connecting hospitality, that "unique trait of humans," with migration,
that "predisposition of the living." Under a balanced
wording, deliberately moving away from the polemics that stir up fear and rejection, their conclusion is
incontrovertible: "Within the ethical goal to ground
humanity in nature, the natural and historical fact of
migration leads to the conclusion that hospitality is
both a philosophical object and a singular characteristic of humans among all living beings."

There is no life without solidarity. This principle is understood even by plants, whose vegetal intelligence never ceases to exist in relationship with

its environment—other plants, the humus of the soil, climatic conditions, and so on.[3] Plants live off each other, surviving in concert and in dialogue, never failing to contradict an antagonistic vision of life. Unfortunately, our own species, blinded by its destructive power, forgets that lesson and believes that survival lies in a retreat into closed identities, shut off from the world with its pluralistic vitality. By constructing a mental wall that distinguishes and separates two natures, one tame and the other threatening, the metaphor of the garden and the jungle is actually nothing but a political variant of social Darwinism. As a betrayal of the work of Charles Darwin, this ideology of the survival of the fittest makes rivalry and competition the rule for life. Yet naturalists since the time of Darwin have taught us that the ideology of winners and victors is contrary to nature.

Every lover and practitioner of nature knows from experience that natural selection is not nature's unequivocal law. The actual law of the jungle is none other than mutual assistance, which was first theorized by the anarchist scholar Pierre Kropotkine.[4] And contrary to the garden, which subdues, dominates, and sometimes impoverishes nature through human authority, the jungle is the universe in all its diversity and robust cooperation. This secret truth was learned from experience and preserved by the

African peoples enslaved during Europe's colonial expansion and cast upon the other side of the Atlantic. In their patient resistance, the weak against the strong, against the totalitarian system of the plantation, they thus invented what came to be known as the creole garden. These traditional gardens, where fruits and vegetables were cultivated, brought together a great variety of different plants in a muddle of apparent disorder. Today, they are studied as pioneering models that impoverished neither the soil nor what grew there. By mixing, combining, and blending, these garden-jungles establish relationship, and not division, as the cardinal principle.

Mutual aid against hatred, cooperation rather than competition, welcome instead of rejection. While our leaders expose their cluelessness, this wisdom is preserved by volunteers, educators, sailors, mountain dwellers, and so on, all those who offer hospitality throughout Europe and go out to meet those seeking refuge. Taking this steep road, the kindhearted people of the highest city in France, Briançon, perched on the French–Italian border, at one point saved the honor of both France and Europe when they were faced with the worst tragedy experienced by migrants, both exiles and refugees, upon our continent since the Second World War. Thanks to the impetus provided by the volunteers of the association Tous Migrants [All migrants], the residents

of Briançon made the practical, pragmatic, and real-
istic demonstration that we are not experiencing a
migration crisis but rather an excess of indifference
and egotism.[5]

During these recent years, this commune in the
high mountains of the Alps has offered hospitality
to a number of migrants that equals the inhabitants
of its capital city, without any notable problems or re-
jections on the part of the residents. This rendezvous
with oneself by welcoming one's neighbors, from however far away they come, has been a benefit for everyone involved, increasing their solidarity, reducing their
isolation, and making them happier and less closed off.
Because it is carried out on the level of the commune,
it is as if this resistance by citizens to the politics of
refusal and rejection, to walls erected by governments,
and to powers that are more and more repressive, less
and less caring for the world, has suddenly restored all
the force and meaning to the word common, that syn-
onym for equality. The common: that which is shared,
that which establishes ties, that which binds and gath-
ers. That which belongs not to an individual but to
everyone. That which is as valuable as gold, gold that
is neither counted up nor spent, subject neither to calculation nor speculation. Gold that is neither bought
nor sold. Gold that is priceless.

If the mountaineers of Tous Migrants, just
like the sailors of the sea rescue organization SOS

Méditerranée, have stepped forward to embrace hospitality, it is because this care for the common is at the burning heart of their experience. This essential knowledge, that no one can survive without the other, is joined to an awareness of dangers and the equally deep emotions that are offered by the landscapes and seascapes where they venture. Unforgettable moments, unlikely solidarity, vertiginous horizons. Without empty words, without useless chatter or vain speeches, their engagement holds the evidence: it tells what they are, namely that they exist in solidarity. And therefore, if they will forgive my grandiloquence, in such uncertain and doubtful times as these, when benevolence and generosity have abandoned the high halls of our states, they are the just of the earth.

Providing a contrast to refrains currently in vogue that celebrate *premiers de cordée*, those elite individuals out front, their actions remind us of the need for *cordées solidaires*, the safety lines, strong and durable, that hold climbers together in solidarity. *Cordée solidaire* was the name given to a memorable initiative organized on December 17, 2017, by Tous Migrants on the Col de l'Échelle pass, between France and Italy, at an elevation of 1,762 meters (5,781 feet), in the region known as the massif of Cerces. In reply, on April 22, 2018, the far right movement Identitarian Generation launched a highly publicized operation for the

"defense of Europe against the migratory invasion."
Two dates that draw a line in the sand.

The history of solidarity is not merely one of women and men showing care for others, whoever they may be and from wherever they may come. More forcibly, this history recounts a keen awareness of the sole path to safety at this moment of the climate countdown, when every living being (*tout vivant*) is in danger, and with them, our entire world (*tout monde*), to borrow terms from Édouard Glissant, the great poet and philosopher of relationship (*relation*).[6] To help one another instead of building up walls with which to barricade ourselves: it is the choice between a political ecology that protects and preserves the common good and an irreversible plunge into a war of all against all.

Just as any people that oppresses another cannot be free, a people that will not step forward to provide basic acts of solidarity to a stranger who seeks asylum will no longer know, when tomorrow comes, how to preserve those values for itself. A culture of every man for himself, of egotism, of apathy, and of callousness—such a renunciation inevitably leads to a general abdication. For behind the question of hospitality lies that of equality: equal rights without any distinction based upon origin, condition, culture, sex, appearance, belief, and so on.

An obsession with security, prompted by the migration question, has caused us to accept the existence of camps in Europe, where people are locked up without having committed any crime, but for simply exercising a natural right articulated in Article 13 of the 1948 Universal Declaration of Human Rights: "Everyone has the right to leave any country, including his own, and to return to his country." This is how we accustom ourselves to infringements of our fundamental rights: the absolute power of a police state, the detention of minors regardless of the rights of childhood, restrictions on the freedom to come and go, restrictions on the freedom of expression and the right to protest, interrogations of the rights of asylum, health, education, and housing, xenophobic speeches and actions, the criminalization of solidarity, scorn for human life, the dehumanization of the Other simply because they are other. In short, we ignore the demands of equality and become accustomed to the arbitrariness of inequality.

Relegated by the defeat of the Nazis and their allies to the margins of public debate and political existence, the far right has worked to regain prominence by using the migration question as its Trojan horse. Migration has been its obsessive refrain in France ever since 1972, when the National Front, which later became the National Rally, was created, with the motto "Stop Rampant Immigration."

Beyond the xenophobia and racism that feeds this anti-immigration obsession, its political objective is to fracture the universal application of rights, and as a result undermine the values, principles, and points of reference of our democratic culture.

Since 1980, thirty-two immigration laws passed in France have not resolved any of the crises this country is facing, be they democratic, social or ecological, ethical or geopolitical. But those laws have succeeded in planting at the heart of the public debate the words and ideas upon which the far right thrives. To know that human rights do not apply for each and every one, that it is legitimate to sort out those possessing rights from those who don't, that it is normal to institute a national preference for the citizens of a state, that we must barricade ourselves against the world that surrounds us, that the stranger is a threat, or even a danger, and that, finally, certain people are a risk to one's identity or one's eternity—that is a summary of the pernicious ideology known as the "great replacement," together with its corollary, "remigration," which is a call to erase, exclude, discriminate, or expel human beings.

It is not only a matter of words. In January 2024, the German investigative journal *Correctiv* revealed that a secret meeting was held on November 25, 2023, in a hotel near Potsdam to discuss plans for the remigration of millions of citizens.[7] Among its participants were political personalities of Alternative for Germany (AfD), the chief German party of the far right, as well as some neo-Nazis. But not just them. Around the table, wealthy entrepreneurs and businessmen rubbed elbows with lawyers and doctors; in short, the elite. The invitation they received openly announced the "global concept, in the sense of a strategic plan," which involved "reversing the installation of foreigners" by organizing the remigration outside of Germany of three targeted groups: asylum-seekers, foreigners with legal residence, and "non-assimilated citizens."

Thus, emphasizes the *Correctiv*'s investigation, "people must be expelled from Germany if they have the wrong skin color, the wrong origin, or if they are not sufficiently 'assimilated.' Even if they are German citizens. It would be an attack upon fundamental law, upon citizenship, and upon the principle of equality." This conspiratorial meeting evokes a European past of sinister memory. Their plan for "remigration" recalls the first project by the National Socialists to deport four million Jews in 1940 to the then-French island of Madagascar, before the Nazi regime decided upon mass extermination. Another sinister coincidence: the hotel chosen by these organizers was located only eight kilometers (five miles) from the villa of the Wannsee Conference, where the Nazis developed the "final solution to the Jewish question."

But it is not only the far right: the anti-immigration obsession of the majority of European governments repeatedly reinforces the idea of separating out undesirable populations, keeping them far away and invisible. In other words, a wish for apartheid. Before being defeated in the general elections held on July 4, 2024, Rishi Sunak, the British Conservative prime minister, got Parliament to pass a bill in an overnight session on April 22. According to the bill, every asylum-seeker entering the United Kingdom illegally, mainly by crossing the English Channel on inflatable boats, would be expelled to Rwanda, at the heart of the African continent, no matter where they had come from. While this general plan of expulsion was abandoned by Sunak's Labour Party successor, a new government in Poland, formed by a center-left alliance with the pro-EU politician Donald Tusk at its head, passed a law on July 12, 2024, that authorized the armed forces to open fire on migrants attempting to enter its territory by crossing the border with Belarus.

At the same time, in the United States, the Heritage Foundation, an ultraconservative think tank that is as influential as it is powerful, has developed, under the title of Project 2025, an all-out attack upon American democracy, taking the rejection of immigration as one of its priorities. Commenting on this "presidential transition project," Mike Davis, who is very close to Donald Trump, did not beat around the bush: "We're gonna deport. We're gonna deport a lot of people, ten million people and growing: anchor babies, their parents, their grandparents. We're gonna put kids in cages. It's gonna be glorious."[8]

Without the same degree of public exuberance, a similar project in France was also unveiled in the summer of 2024. Financed by a billionaire working to elect Marine Le Pen as president, this project elevated immigration, together with "wokeism," as its prime target, with plans to dedicate 65 percent of the first sums invested in a campaign for this far right candidate to these two "principal evils of France." The project's title, PERICLES—standing for Patriots, Native [*Enracinés*], Resisters, Identitarians, Christians, Libertarians, Europeans, and Sovereigntists—leaves nothing to doubt. So many symbols—including the acronym, taken from the Athenian strategist from antiquity—that proclaim a war not only against the foreigner who comes from elsewhere, but also against the world that is within us, the melting pot of our societies and our diversity.[9]

Building to a mortifying crescendo, anti-immigration policies have brought about a brutalization of our societies, our humanistic values, and our democratic principles. The migrant question is thus none other than the question of who we are. To close oneself off from others is to close oneself off from oneself. Our relationship to the distant dictates our vision of our neighbor—at least if we lay claim to emancipation, that infinite journey, never fully achieved, toward liberation from servitudes and oppressions. Any attempt to negotiate with the politics of exclusion, national preference, or identitarian boundaries throws in the towel, empowering the far right, with their inequality, identitarianism, and authoritarianism.

From this perspective, the idea of movement, that fundamental right to circulate, resonates well beyond migrants, refugees, and exiles. Every politics of equality is in effect a politics of movement: it is the right not to be assigned a domicile, but to be able to make one's way, to escape, to choose one's own destiny and seek new horizons. There's no need for a great voyage to understand this concept: to escape domination of every kind—class, sex, origin, and so on—that divides and oppresses humanity is what it means to achieve the right to move. To go and see other places. To pick oneself up and go. To make one's way freely.

In this sense, the heroes who seek hospitality after coming from Syria, Sudan, Afghanistan, Iraq, and so many other countries speak to us of our own emancipations by means of the fires they have escaped or passed through. The movement that they claim for themselves—surmounting walls, barbed wire, police, armies, detention centers, expulsions, tracking, persecutions—reminds us that we are also the fruit and the beneficiaries of movement, achieved through great struggle, sometimes in tragedy and often in hope, by the generations that preceded us.

To defend their right to move is to defend our own. To save them is to save our own soul, the soul of Europe. Unfortunately, the official policies of Europe today are moving in the opposite direction, away from a policy of hospitality. The "promotion of our European way of life" once fell within the portfolio of the European commissioner who oversees migration questions, just as, in France, the presidency of Nicolas Sarkozy combined immigration and "national identity" under the same ministry. In the initial wording of the European ministry, it even phrased it as the "*protection* of our European way of life," thereby associating issues of immigration—that is, men and women who come from elsewhere and are exercising their fundamental right to movement— with the defense of some idealized and fantasized European identity, which those movements of people call into question and put at risk.

Through semantic slippages that enshroud the criminalization of hospitality and solidarity, the European Union thus comes to accept, normalize, and disseminate racist and xenophobic rhetoric. By citing a "European mode of life" as evidence, it implies that the Other who sets out, requests hospitality, seeks a better life, tries to escape the random chance of birth, flees social injustices, denials of democracy, violent chaos, or climate disasters, the Other who moves to shape their own destiny, according to their dreams and ambitions, exercising a fundamental right guaranteed by the Universal Declaration of Human Rights, and imitating what European peoples have done and still do by launching themselves upon the world and voyaging to all the continents—that this Other is therefore an existential threat.

Meanwhile, the truth of European history—the creation of its wealth and the building of the continent's power, with strength that is both economic and intellectual, demographic as well as cultural—shows that Europe was fashioned, produced, and invented through its encounter, sometimes violent, with the world's diverse populations. Moreover, is there but one "way of life" in Europe? On its own, this single expression manages to preclude social questions by asserting identitarian ones. What mode of life is common to all of Europe's countries, when their populations are crisscrossed by inequalities of revenue, access to education, health, and public services, housing conditions, ability to relocate, and so on? Coming from on high, is this expression of a common civilizational identity, which obliterates social distinctions, anything other than an ideological trick meant to obfuscate the inescapable question of the appropriation of wealth in the hands of a minority at levels not seen since the late nineteenth century?

Clearly, to persist in using the language of a continent, a civilization, and peoples who believe themselves to be superior to others, who feel justified in barricading themselves within their certainty of being good and just, means that one has learned nothing from the history of modern Europe. How is that any different from the identitarian speeches which today mark the xenophobic nationalisms everywhere in the world, always wrapped in a defense of culture, whether in New Delhi, Beijing, or Moscow, in Riyadh or Ankara, in Buenos Aires or Washington? No people, no nation, no continent, and no civilization can claim sole possession of the universal. Worse, this same claim contains its own negation, in that it implies that there are hierarchies between cultures, origins, and identities. By espousing the ideology of a clash of civilizations, such claims create a self-fulfilling prophecy and hasten the world's march toward confrontation, conflict, and disorder.

In this sense, the desire to "promote our European way of life" does nothing but ordain and prolong Europe's renunciation of its own values, as we see in the language of its leaders, who are so painfully managing the migration issues. "The European Union needs more humane borders," declared Ursula von der Leyen in Strasbourg in 2019, during her first address to the European parliament; she was reelected in 2024 as president of the European Commission. The statement is a disgrace. For if the Mediterranean, our common sea, has become an aquatic cemetery, it is very much the fault of Europe, which through Frontex has erected a border and a wall instead of an access road, a passage to form ties, a place of sharing and relation.

It is in this way that Europe silently enacts a pedagogy of separating human beings, of keeping others at a distance by erasing and expelling them. And this is the way that a new political jungle invades its so-called garden.

8 ▸ THE TRIUMPH OF DEATH

THE PALAIS DE LA Porte Dorée, which today houses a museum on the history of immigration, was originally a museum of the colonies, built on the occasion of the International Colonial Exhibition of 1931. When visiting its permanent exhibit, you discover a large map of Europe and its immediate geographic surroundings, showing only dots made of a scarlet red. Each of these red circles represents, according to size, a number of individuals who died or went missing, between 2014 and 2022, during their migration to Europe. Like so many drops of blood. At the center of the map, they come together to form a sea of blood that wraps itself entirely around Sicily and the islands, such as Lampedusa, that belong to this region of the Italian republic.

"Adam, where are you?...Where is your brother?...Where is the blood of your brother?"[1] It was in Lampedusa that on July 8, 2013, Pope Francis posed these questions to the world, and in particular to Europe. You do not need to be a believer—I am not one myself—to see yourself in these words of humanity that have become so rare in the political discourse of Europe. Yes, what have we done with our brothers and our sisters, with our humanity? "This is not a question directed to others; it is a question directed to me, to you, to each of us," said the head of the Catholic Church. "These brothers and sisters of ours were trying to escape difficult situations to find some serenity and peace; they were looking for a better place for themselves and their families, but instead they found death. How often do such people fail to find understanding, fail to find acceptance, fail to find solidarity." Ten years later, on September 22, 2023, this same Jesuit pope from the Southern Hemisphere reiterated this appeal in Marseille, in front of a memorial to sailors and migrants lost at sea. "We can no longer watch the drama of shipwrecks, caused by...the fanaticism of indifference," he declared, establishing that to rescue those seeking refuge is a "duty of civilization."[2]

Between the garden and the jungle, where is civilization to be found? That's the very word, elusive and overused, that the Israeli prime minister, Benjamin Netanyahu, invoked on May 30, 2024, as he tried to rally France, and all of Europe, to his cause.

On the news channel of a major French media company, Netanyahu declared, "Our victory is your victory! It's the victory of Judeo-Christian civilization over barbarity. It's the victory of France!"[3] Strange words coming from someone facing the possibility of an arrest warrant by the International Criminal Court for war crimes and crimes against humanity.

This media episode does nothing to cast the state of France in a favorable light, nor its dominant media and its current government, whose obvious complacency toward the extremist ruling power in Israel has contrasted with the tireless mobilization of the youth in solidarity with the people of Gaza. On the day before this televised interview, the newspaper *Haaretz* gave visual representation, through the use of black redactions, to the censorship imposed on it by a government whose prime minister had not granted a single interview to the Israeli media since the massacres of October 7, 2023, fearing to take questions from journalists who would be more aggressive and critical. Netanyahu's interview took place in France to prevent that country from recognizing the State of Palestine, unlike Spain, Ireland, Norway, and Slovenia, which in 2024 joined nine other European states that have taken the lead in this defense of equal rights on the diplomatic landscape.[4] On the other side, the German government elevated the Israeli cause to a "reason of state," while the president of the National Assembly in France did not hesitate in confirming his "unconditional" support for the State of Israel—where "unconditional" signifies the abdication of full critical clarity. Finally, in this same dishonorable chain of events, the former president of France, Nicolas Sarkozy, took his turn for an interview to proclaim the "Judeo-Christian roots" of Europe as part of a diatribe against "decolonialism" and "*islamo-gauchisme*," a term of abuse used by the right to equate the political left with Islamic fundamentalism.[5]

This "Judeo-Christian" mantra is the refrain of advocates of the clash of civilizations, who promote Israel, that "villa in the jungle," as an outpost of Europe, confronting the Muslim world like a kind of citadel on the front lines. But that claim is a lie of history, an Islamophobic myth that ignores centuries of anti-Semitism in the West. It is also a sinister reversal: after almost two millennia of European persecutions fueled by Chistian anti-Judaism, the Jews, whether in Israel or the diaspora, were thus brought in as a pledge, serving as both alibi and shield for an anti-Muslim and anti-Arab crusade. Even when that means denying the pluralism of the Palestinian people, whose Christian component was always represented within the Palestinian Liberation Organization (PLO) and championed by its founder, Yasser Arafat, in opposition to the Islamist ideology of Hamas.

Against Benjamin Netanyahu and his confederates, let us turn to Jules Isaac (1877–1963), who is forever linked in France to the educational tracts of Malet-Isaac, the famous history textbook that he wrote during France's Third Republic (1870–1940). Isaac is as forgotten today as he was pivotal to the cause of Jewish-Christian reconciliation after the Second World War and the European catastrophe. "Must I apologize for continuing to fight to remove, and if possible, uproot the Christian roots of anti-Semitism? No, because in my opinion, those roots run deepest."[6] Such are the opening words of *The Teaching of Contempt* (1962), published one year before the death of its author, and following his earlier books, *Jesus and Israel* (1948) and *Has Anti-Semitism Roots in Christianity?* (1956).

A pro-Dreyfus friend of Charles Péguy and a professor of history who was named inspector general of public education in 1936 before becoming a victim of the Jewish persecutions starting in 1940, Jules Isaac would dedicate the final twenty years of his life "to dissecting, exposing, and combating the Christian roots of anti-Semitism," according to his biographer, André Kaspi, by founding in 1948 the organization l'Amitié judéo-chrétienne [Jewish-Christian Friendship].[7] That was the year that Isaac published *Jesus and Israel*, the goal of which was simply "to confront the Christian world with its responsibilities, which are heavy."[8] The book is dedicated to his wife and daughter, murdered in Auschwitz, "killed by Hitler's Nazis, killed simply because their name was Isaac."[9]

From books to conferences, even in Rome, before Pope John XXIII during the ecumenical council of Vatican II, Isaac went on pleading tirelessly for a recognition of the *longue durée* of Christian anti-Semitism, which formed a fertile European soil for the crime of the Nazis. Meticulously reconstructing how a minoritarian (and revolutionary) branch within Judaism was transmuted into the institution of a Christian church that would reach the summit of power, he shows how Christianity got turned around in its quest for power over its Jewish origins. That explains, he writes in his unpublished *Leper's Notebook*, composed during the German occupation, how he arrived at his "conviction, that this received tradition, taught for hundreds and hundreds of years by thousands and thousands of voices, was the first source of anti-Semitism, the sturdy, secular stump upon which all the other varieties of anti-Semitism—even the most contrary— would come to be grafted."[10]

"I say and maintain," declared Isaac during a conference in December 1959 at the Sorbonne University in Paris, "that the death-dealing racialism of our time, though in its essence anti-Christian, has developed in Christian soil, and that it has carefully harvested the heritage, the very dubious heritage, of

Christianity."[11] This legacy, particularly the accusation of deicide, flourished as soon as church and state were united in the Roman Empire. "For eighteen hundred years," writes Isaac as a summary of the pivotal chapter of *Jesus and Israel*, "it has been generally taught throughout the Christian world that the Jewish people, in full responsibility for the Crucifixion, committed the inexpiable crime of deicide. No accusation could be more pernicious—and in fact none has caused more innocent blood to be shed."[12]

A thousand miles from the irenic myth of a shared Judeo-Christian civilization, this Christian prejudice guided centuries of anti-Jewish persecution before leading to the modern genocide of the Jews of Europe. In 1096, the First Crusade, proclaimed the previous year by Pope Urban II at the Council of Clermont, began with pogroms in which Jews were murdered and baptized by force, and their property was seized, primarily in Rouen and Metz but also in Germany. In 1215, the Fourth Lateran Council intensified the anti-Jewish position, particularly by requiring Jews to wear distinctive clothing and excluding them from holding public office. In 1269, King Louis IX of France compelled Jews to wear a roundel, a small wheel of yellow fabric sewn onto their coat, the precursor of the yellow star of the Nazi persecutions.[13]

Moving on to the invention of the ghetto in Venice, the physical separation of the Jews in the Middle Ages first involved a prohibition against appearing in public on Sundays and during Holy Week, the week before Easter. Later, it culminated in outright expulsions that expanded in the same degree that Europe projected itself upon the world. Coinciding with the first transatlantic expedition of Christopher Columbus, who departed Spain on August 3, 1492, the Jews had been forced to leave Spain by July 31 of that same year, according to a decree of the Catholic monarchs Isabelle and Ferdinand, who had just captured Granada and brought an end to eight centuries of Islam in the West. This was the Catholic Spain of the Reconquista, which a century later would similarly expel the Moriscos from their country in 1609, the Muslims forcibly converted to Catholicism.[14]

The expulsion from Spain, followed by Portugal in 1496, was the final rejection for the Jews of the continent, following their banishment from nearly everywhere else, including England in 1290 and France in 1306. During this long era of European history, the persecution of Jews became part of the affirmation of a hegemonic and homogeneous Christian identity that hunted down every instance of the Other and legitimized its own supremacy. The concept of "blood purity," *limpieza de sangre*, dominated the Iberian Peninsula from the fifteenth through the nineteenth century, pursuing every Jewish or Moorish bloodline, even as the onset of globalization, launched with the conquest of the American continent, forced Europe to encounter the Other and confront the question of pluralistic identities—which is to say the intermixing of races.

When, under King Louis XIV, the Black Code of 1685 codified slavery in the Antilles, its first article demanded the expulsion of "the Jews who have taken up residence there," on the charge that they were "avowed enemies of the Christian name." Later, the same Napoleon I, who reinstituted slavery in 1802 after it had been abolished by the French Revolution, was also the one who established a new Christian monarchy, implicitly depriving the Jews of the citizenship they acquired in 1791 by subjecting them to special laws that defined them as other, different, agitators, "a nation within a nation," as the emperor summed it up, intoning the words that would subsequently become the chorus of the modern anti-Semites, particularly Édouard Drumont, Charles Maurras, and Action Française.

The recent invention of a "Judeo-Christian civilization," which asserts a cultural homogeneity that excludes the Muslim component of European history, had as figurehead one of their contemporaries and elders, Ernest Renan. Having provided scholarly legitimacy to the distinction between Aryans and Semites, itself imaginary and inherited from German Orientalism, Renan divided Semites into Jews and Muslims in the context of the imperial expansion of colonialism and its confrontation with Islam. The annexation of Judaism to a superior Christian civilization would serve Renan in the argument for a civilizational exclusion of Islam.

Olivier Le Cour Grandmaison has extensively documented the fundamental Islamophobia of Renan, who was convinced that Europe was on its way to an absolute conquest of the world, when the West would finally take its revenge on the Muslims of the East.[15] "For human reason, Islam has been only harmful," wrote Renan in 1883,[16] echoing his words from twenty years earlier on February 21, 1862, to the Collège de France, when he proclaimed, "The European genius is developing with a greatness beyond compare. Islamism, by contrast, is slowly decomposing; in our time, it has come crashing down. At present, the necessary condition for the spread of European civilization is the destruction of the Semitic par excellence, the destruction of the theocratic power of Islamism, and as a result, the destruction of Islamism."[17]

Be careful here about any anachronistic misunderstanding: the Islam of which he speaks here has barely any connection with the totalitarian and terrorist ideologies which today lay claim to Islam, despite being filled with racist prejudice against the peoples that they are dominating, the cultures they are destroying, and the territories they are conquering. Notice also how the propaganda of Benjamin Netanyahu, in our own time, invokes the same vision for the service of a similar political goal: "We are part of European culture…Europe ends in Israel," he said as early as 2017 to an audience of European leaders, seeking to appoint Israel as the vanguard of Judeo-Christian civilization.

Toby Greene, professor at Bar-Ilan University in Israel, recalls Netanyahu's declaration in a 2020 article about the political instrumentalization of the term "Judeo-Christian" by the far right. He goes on to underscore how this ideological weapon fans the flames of a terrible clash of civilizations in which humanity runs toward the abyss, caught between two fires: "The radical right claim that Europe's Judeo-Christian values are incompatible with Islam reinforces the parallel claim of Islamists, who seek to persuade Muslims that the west and Islam are inherently in conflict."[18]

For the epigraph to his book *The Teaching of Contempt: Christian Roots of Anti-Semitism*, Jules Isaac selects two quotations. One is from his teacher and friend Charles Péguy: "There is something worse than having an evil mind, and that is having a closed one." The other is from his Christian interlocutor, the reformist pope John XXIII: "It is a fundamental rule of life never to distort the truth."[19] In 1955, at the height of the Cold War, confronted with the arms race and the atomic era, Isaac wrote to Albert Einstein to propose that he establish a "committee on public health for the defense of humanity."[20] The scientist died before being able to reply. But we who are still living can say how welcome this initiative would be at a moment when humanity is dying, right before our very eyes, in Gaza. How it dies in every place—Ukraine, Syria, Yemen, and others—where the rights and the equality of human beings are scorned by powers and potentates, by civilizations and religions, by nations and identities, that declare themselves superior to others.

The island of Lampedusa, whose name is forever tied to the fate of migrants in the Mediterranean, belongs administratively to the region of Sicily, with Palermo as its capital. The botanic garden of this regional capital, planted in 1789, at the same time as the French Revolution, formerly housed a colonial garden. It runs along the Kalsa district, a name of Arabic origin, like many other names in these ancient places of connection and blending, meeting and mingling. The Kalsa is home to the Palazzo Abatellis, where you can contemplate Palermo's most famous painting, *The Triumph of Death*. This immense fresco, dating to the mid-fifteenth century, depicts Death astride a gaunt horse as he indiscriminately fells the living with his arrows. Emperors, popes, bishops, knights—all the powerful of their day—pass from life to death, while on the right of the scene, a group of nobles, richly dressed and oblivious to the inexorable fate that awaits them, carries on with detached indifference.

This work of art does not strike me as belonging to yesterday: it is our own mirror today, showing a Europe that is rushing toward its own destruction.

9 ▸ HUMANITY AND THE EARTH

"THE EARTH IS THE blood of the dead," according to Kanak tradition in New Caledonia. "The earth is the body of humanity," echoes Élisée Reclus in a prophetic warning from 1864 about the risks that humans pose to nature, speaking neither of the garden nor the jungle, but merely our shared, fleeting passage through this world, before death returns us to the womb of the living.

I owe the discovery of this ancient oceanic wisdom to the anthropologist Jean Guiart, who makes these observations: "The land is composed of the blood of the dead, and we want this land because we need to be able to come face-to-face, once again, with our dead, who constitute the foundation of our society and our essential tradition, as well as the link that binds us to the land that they compose. Such is the profound conviction, endlessly repeated in all manner of forms, of the New Caledonia Melanesians, who today wish to be called the Kanak people."[1]

Élisée Reclus would have been able to discover that same belief in New Caledonia, or Kanaky, if his sentence of deportation there for participating in the Paris Commune of 1871 had been carried out. Under the pressure of an international petition from scientists, among them Charles Darwin, the founder of the theory of evolution, his sentence was commuted to ten years' banishment. Yet Reclus did not need to be alerted to this immemorial knowledge from the other side of the world in order to formulate it for himself, for in his life and work, he never stopped standing up against the deliriums of power and the frenzies of domination by our species. It is to this towering libertarian geographer that the French language owes the invention of the term *l'entraide*, which Reclus suggested to the French translator of a book first published in English in 1902 by Pierre Kropotkine, *Mutual Aid: A Factor of Evolution*.[2]

"We are the sons of the earth," as Reclus wrote in 1864 in an article in *Revue des deux mondes*,[3] sparked by reading *Man and Nature*, a momentous book published that year by George Perkins Marsh, considered to be the first American ecologist.[4] "Whatever the relative degree of freedom won through intelligence and exercise of the will, we nevertheless remain mere products of the planet," cautions Reclus, before inviting man, "this new Atila," to become aware of his responsibility toward the living of the world, at a time when "human works unfortunately have had the fatal result of impoverishing the soil, disfiguring nature, and wrecking climates."

Humanity and the Earth, Reclus's last book, appeared after his death in 1905 in Torhout, Belgium, not far from Bruges.[5] His final pages are dedicated to a critique of progress and of the civilizations that proclaim themselves to be its proprietors, against whom he introduces the dialectically intertwined concept of regress. It is an appeal for the solidarity he considers the wellspring of a true human progress and a means to escape, he writes, from "our demi-civilization, only a demi-civilization because it does not benefit everyone."[6] He concludes with an invitation to "cultivate our earthly garden": "To show favor upon each individual life of plant, animal, or man, to become fully aware of our united humanity, to become one with the planet itself, to behold our origins, our present, our approaching goal, our distant ideal—that is where progress lies."[7]

The Extraordinary Voyages, a series of novels by Jules Verne, makes a tour around the world that Europe believed itself to have mastered by the end of the nineteenth century, when the novels were written. Verne's novels owe much to the nineteen-volume geographic encyclopedia of Élisée Reclus, from which the author, who had scarcely traveled, drew a great quantity of material. The heroes of Verne's *Voyage to the Center of the Earth* depart from Iceland and travel from one volcano to another, arriving on August 31 in Sicily, after having been cast from the entrails of the earth upon the slopes of the Aeolian Island of Stromboli.

This island volcano also fascinated another writer, Alexandre Dumas, the author of *The Count of Monte Cristo* and *The Three Musketeers*, who was himself born from the history that I wish to invoke in this book. Dumas's father was born in Saint-Domingue (today, Haiti) as the son of an enslaved woman. During the French Revolution, he became the heroic General Dumas and even served for a time as commander in chief of the army of the Alps. According to the account of his father that Alexandre Dumas writes in his memoirs, this devil of a man was not afraid to stand up to Napoleon during the Egyptian campaign. Dumas summarizes their confrontation in terms—who knows how true to life—that emphasize the noxiousness of Caesarism, the power of a single person to subsume the will of all:

"I think that the interests of France ought to come before those of an individual, no matter how great that man may be," declared General Dumas. "I do not think that the fortunes of any nation should be subordinated to those of an individual."

"So you are ready to separate yourself from me?" asked Bonaparte.

"Yes, so soon as I am convinced that you are separating yourself from France."

"You are mistaken, Dumas," Bonaparte replied coldly.

"Quite possibly," replied my father, "but I disapprove of dictatorships—whether those of Sulla or of Caesar."[8]

For Dumas, Stromboli, a mountain he had once climbed, was a metaphor of revolutions, those unforeseeable uprisings that sometimes succeed in interrupting a race into the abyss. In the context of the Springtime of Nations in 1848, with France's February Revolution at its epicenter, he identified that volcano with France, which, he wrote, "is like steam: the more you compress it, the closer it comes to exploding. Across from Russia and England, France is only an atom. Stromboli too is only a single point, but it contains a volcano. It's called the 'Lighthouse of the Mediterranean.' Like Stromboli, France is, by turns, lighthouse and volcano."[9]

I wish I could believe it. But when I observe expanding shadows and threatening darkness, I am not so sure. In May 2022, an enormous wildfire laid waste to the slopes of Stromboli, weakening its soil to the point of allowing, three months later, a massive mudslide after a meteorological bomb dropped a deluge of water. The cause of this blaze was not the volcano, but man. Not nature, but our own species. It was, in fact, the filming of an episode of a sensationalist show—hosted by Italian public television channel RAI, and ironically about the Department of Civil Protection—that caused a conflagration on a scale never before caused by an eruption of Stromboli. This true history is a modern fable on the nature of man, hazardous not only for the life of the world but also for himself, due to his pretensions to rule and dominate all, to appropriate and exploit everything.

True progress, returning to the observations of Élisée Reclus, would consist in impeding this kind of man. "To be a man is to restrain oneself," as Albert Camus makes his father say in his posthumous novel *The First Man*. Which is another way of saying that the absence of limits is the source of toxicity for our species, for its male leaders, as crazy about themselves as about their vainglorious, power-obsessed nations, and, above all for the ruling classes, greedy for riches and never satisfied.

A man caught between two worlds, Africa and Europe, a libertarian too little known, who knew only one homeland, the French language, Camus was already speaking of us in 1957, in his acceptance speech of the Nobel Prize for Literature: "Each generation doubtless feels called upon to reform the world. Mine knows that it will not reform it, but its task is perhaps even greater. It consists in preventing the world from destroying itself."[10]

That's where we are now, at a moment when the basis of our shared humanity—the universal equality of rights—is radically called into question.

NOTES

1. THE BRUGES SPEECH

1 See Fernand Braudel, *Civilisation matérielle, économie et capitalisme,* xve-xviiie *siècle*, vol. 2, *Les Jeux de l'échange* (Paris: Armand Colin, 1979), 78. *Civilization and Capitalism, 15th–18th Century, Vol. II: The Wheels of Commerce*, trans. Siân Reynold (Oakland: University of California Press, 1992).

2 Joseph Conrad, *Heart of Darkness*, (n.p.: Standard Ebooks, 2014 [1899]).

3 See David Van Reybrouck, *Congo: The Epic History of a People*, trans. Sam Garrett (New York: HarperCollins, 2014).

4 Josep Borrell, "European Diplomatic Academy: Opening Remarks by High Representative Josep Borrell at the Inauguration of the Pilot Programme," European Union External Action, October 13, 2022, https://www.eeas.europa.eu/eeas/european-diplomatic-academy-opening-remarks-high-representative-josep-borrell-inauguration-pilot_en/.

5 "Le Grand Continent–A conversation with the HR/VP," European Union External Action, October 31, 2022, https://www.eeas.europa.eu/eeas/le-grand-continent-conversation-hrvp_en/.

6   Josep Borrell Fontelles, "Europe Between Two Wars," Groupe d'études géopolitiques, January 3, 2024, https://geopolitique.eu/en/2024/01/03/europe-between-two-wars/.

7   Renaud Girard, "Benyamin Netanyahou au *Figaro*: 'C'est une guerre de civilisation!'" LCRS Politica, June 19, 2024.

8   See Edwy Plenel, *L'Appel à la vigilance* (Paris: La Découverte, 2023).

9   Gustave Le Bon, *The Crowd: A Study of the Popular Mind* (New York: Macmillan, 1897), 101.

10   Victor Klemperer, *The Language of the Third Reich: LTI, Lingua Tertii Imperii: A Philologist's Notebook*, trans. Martin Brady (London: A & C Black, 2006), 14.

11   Robert Kagan, *The Jungle Grows Back: America and Our Imperiled World* (New York: Vintage Books, 2018).

12   Diogenes Candle, "Contextualizing Zone of Interest," *Diogenes's Newsletter* (blog), April 22, 2024, https://diogenescandle.substack.com/p/contextualizing-the-zone-of-interest/.

13   See Rudolf Hoess, *Commandant of Auschwitz: The Autobiography of Rudolf Hoess*, trans. Constantine Fitzgibbon (London: Phoenix Press, 2000).

2. THE BATTLE FOR RIGHTS

1   Immanuel Kant, *Critique of Judgement*, 2nd ed., rev., trans. J. H. Bernard (London: Macmillan, 1914). See Jacques Rancière, *The Time of the Landscape: On the Origins of the Aesthetic Revolution*, trans. Emiliano Battista (Cambridge: Polity Press, 2023).

2   Immanuel Kant, "Physical Geography." In Eric Watkins (ed.), *Natural Science* (Cambridge: Cambridge University Press, 2012b), 434–678.

3   Kant, "Physical Geography," 505.

4   Kant, "Physical Geography," 660.

5   Kant, "Physical Geography," 641.

6   Kant, "Physical Geography," 651.

7   Kant, "Physical Geography," 669.

8   Kant, "Physical Geography," 655.

9   Kant, "Physical Geography," 576.

10 Immanuel Kant, *Kant: Political Writings*, ed. H. S. Reiss, trans. H. B. Nisbet, 2nd ed. of Cambridge Texts in the History of Political Thought (Cambridge: Cambridge University Press, 1991), 107–8.

11 Immanuel Kant, *Vers la paix perpétuelle*, introduction by Françoise Proust, trans. Jean-François Poirier and Françoise Proust (Paris: GF Flammarion, 1991), 96.

12 "The crisis," Gramsci writes in 1930, "consists precisely in the fact that the old is dying and the new cannot be born; in this interregnum a great variety of morbid symptoms appear." See Antonio Gramsci, *Prison Notebooks*, vol. 2, notebook 3, ed. and trans. Joseph A. Buttigieg (New York: Columbia University Press, 2011).

13 ". . . to deliver the world to the assassins of dawn is out of the question": Aimé Césaire, "New Kindness," *The Complete Poetry of Aimé Césaire: Bilingual Edition*, trans. A. James Arnold and Clayton Eshleman (Middletown, CT: Wesleyan University Press, 2017), 791.

14 Alexis Feertchak, "Emmanuel Kant, responsable de la guerre en Ukraine, selon le gouverneur russe de Kaliningrad," *Le Figaro*, February 12, 2024.

15 See Marlène Laruelle, "Dés-occidentaliser le monde: la doctrine Karaganov," *Le Grand Continent*, April 20, 2024.

16 See François Bonnet, "Poutine, un fascisme construit dans le silence des tombes et des cachots," *Mediapart*, February 17, 2024.

17 See Hannah Arendt, *Il n'y a qu'un seul droit de l'homme* précédé de *Nous réfugiés*, trans. Emmanuel Alloa (Paris: Payot, 2021).

3. THEIR HATRED OF EQUALITY

1 Gérard Bonet, *L'Agence Inter-France de Pétain à Hitler. Une entreprise de manipulation de la presse de province* (Paris: Le Félin, 2021).

2 Dominique Sordet, *Les Derniers jours de la démocratie* (Paris: Inter-France, 1944).

3 https://research.calvin.edu/german-propaganda-archive/hitler1
.htm

4 Karl Marx and Frederick Engels, *Manifesto of the Communist Party*, trans. Samuel Moore, 2nd ed. (NY: National Executive Committee of the Socialist Labor Party, 1898 [1888]), 16.

5 Éric Vuillard, *The Order of the Day*, trans. Mark Polizzotti (New York: Other Press, 2018).

6 Zeev Sternhell, *The Anti-Enlightenment Tradition*, trans. David Maisel (New Haven, CT: Yale University Press, 2009).

7 Isaiah Berlin, *Freedom and Its Betrayal: Six Enemies of Human Liberty*, ed. Henry Hardy (Princeton: Princeton University Press, 2003), 153.

8 Joseph de Maistre, *Considerations on France*, trans. Richard A. Lebrun (Cambridge: Cambridge University Press, 1994), 97.

9 Joseph de Maistre, from a letter to his daughter, Mademoiselle Constance de Maistre, 1808. In *Lettres*, 146. https://en.wikiquote .org/wiki/Joseph_de_Maistre

10 Joseph de Maistre, *Against Rousseau: On the State of Nature and On the Sovereignty of the People*, ed. and trans. Richard A. Lebrun (Montreal and Kingston: McGill-Queen's University Press, 1996), 73–74.

11 Saverio Lodato and Roberto Scarpinato, *Il ritorno del principe* (Milan: Chiarelettere, 2008).

12 Eyquem Pons, "Joseph de Maistre: le droit des nations contre les droits de l'homme," *Éléments*, May 10, 2023, https://www .revue-elements.com/joseph-de-maistre-le-droit-des-nations -contre-les-droits-de-lhomme/.

13 Joseph de Maistre, *The Pope, Considered in His Relations with the Church, Temporal Sovereignties, Separated Churches, and the Cause of Civilization*, trans. Aeneas McDonald Dawson (London: C. Dolman, 1850), 292.

14 Paul-François Paoli, "Jean-Louis Harouel: 'Sortons du dogme égalitaire'," *Le Figaro*, January 30, 2024.

15 Jean-Louis Harouel, *Les Mensonges de l'égalité. Ce mal qui ronge la France et l'Occident* (Paris: L'Artilleur, 2023); Jean-Louis Harouel, *Essai sur l'inégalité* (Paris: PUF, 1984).

16 Jean-Louis Harouel, *Les Droits de l'homme contre le peuple* (Paris: Desclée de Brouwer, 2016).

17 See Justine Lacroix and Jean-Yves Pranchère, *Le Procès des droits de l'homme. Généalogie du scepticisme démocratique* (Paris: Seuil, 2016.

4. TURNING THE WORLD UPSIDE DOWN

1 Quoted in "Ecology: Today's Battleground," *Green European Journal*, June 13, 2023, https://www.greeneuropeanjournal.eu/ecology-todays-battleground/.

2 Guillaume Blanc, *The Invention of Green Colonialism*, trans. Helen Morrison (Cambridge, UK: Polity Press, 2022), 1–2.

3 Blanc, *The Invention of Green Colonialism*, 12.

4 Raphael Lemkin, "Genocide," *American Scholar*, vol. 15, no. 2 (April 1946), 227–30.

5 Fanon, Frantz, *The Wretched of the Earth*, trans. Constance Farrington (New York: Grove Press, 1963), 255.

6 Aimé Césaire, *Discours sur le colonialism* (Paris: Présence Africaine, 1955).

7 Frantz Fanon, *Black Skin, White Masks*, trans. Richard Philcox (New York: Grove Press, 2008), 206.

8 Fanon, *Black Skin, White Masks*, 101.

9 Fanon, *Black Skin, White Masks*, 101.

10 Fanon, *Black Skin, White Masks*, 64.

11 Fanon, *The Wretched of the Earth*, 252.

5. THE COLONIAL QUESTION

1 See Elvire de Brissac, *Le Jardin des Plantes ou De l'horrible danger de la promenade* (Paris: Grasset, 2024).

2 See Daniel Schneidermann, *Cinq têtes coupées. Massacres coloniaux. Enquête sur la fabrication de l'oubli* (Paris: Seuil, 2023).

3 See Claude Blanckaert, ed., *La Vénus hottentote: Entre Barnum et Muséum* (Paris: Muséum national d'histoire naturelle, coll. Archives, 2013).

4 Michel Foucault, *Discipline and Punish: The Birth of the Prison*, trans. Alan Sheridan (New York: Vintage Books, 1979), 205.

5   See Sudhir Hazareesingh, *Black Spartacus: The Epic Life of Toussaint Louverture* (London: Allen Lane, 2019).

6   See Fabrice Riceputi, *Le Pen et la torture. Alger 1957, l'histoire contre l'oubli* (Paris: Le Passager clandestin, 2024).

7   Cris Beauchemin, Christelle Hamel and Patrick Simon, eds., *Trajectoires et origines. Enquête sur la diversité des populations en France* (Paris: INED, coll. Grandes enquêtes, 2016).

8   Jean-Claude Guillebaud, *Les Confettis de l'empire* (Paris: Seuil, coll. L'histoire immédiate, 1976).

9   Pierre Nora and Lawrence D. Kritzman, eds., *Realms of Memory: The Construction of the French Past*, 3 vols., trans. Arthur Goldhammer (New York: Columbia University Press, 1996–1998).

10 Marcel Detienne, *L'Identité nationale, une énigme* (Paris: Gallimard, 2010).

11 Patrick Boucheron, *Histoire mondiale de la France* (Paris: Seuil, 2017).

12 Patrick Boucheron and Stéphane Gerson, eds., *France in the World: A New Global History* (New York: Other Press, 2019), 362.

13 See, in *France in the World*, the following contributions: Jean-Frédéric Schaub, "1683: 1492, French-Style?" 357; Manuel Covo, "1791: Plantations in Revolution," 448; in *Histoire Mondiale de la France*: Sylvain Venayre, "1882: Professer la nation," 697.

14 Hannah Arendt, *The Origins of Totalitarianism* (HarperCollins, [1951], 1973).

15 Enzo Traverso, *The Origins of Nazi Violence*, trans. Janet Lloyd (New York: New Press, 2003), 8–9.

16 Traverso, *The Origins of Nazi Violence*, 19.

17 See Aimé Césaire, "Letter to Maurice Thorez," *Social Text* (2010) 28 [2 (103)]: 145–52.

18 Ernest Renan, "8. Intellectual and Moral Reform in France (*La Réforme intellectuelle et morale de la France*, 1871)," in *What Is a Nation? and Other Political Writings*, ed. and trans. M. F. N. Giglioli (New York and Chichester, West Sussex: Columbia University Press, 2018), 232.

19 Aimé Césaire, *Discourse on Colonialism*, trans. Joan Pinkham (New York: Monthly Review Press, 1972), 40.

20 Césaire, *Discourse on Colonialism*, 36.

21 Césaire, *Discourse on Colonialism*, 37.

22 Césaire, *Discourse on Colonialism*, 31.

23 Fanon, *Black Skin, White Masks*, 206.

24 Louise Michel, *Légendes canaques*, preface by Stéphane Mangin (Paris, Éditions Cartouche, 2006).

25 Louise Michel, *Mémoires de Louise Michel, écrits par elle-même* (Paris: Roy, 1886), 289 & 359.

6. A VILLA IN THE JUNGLE

1 Stéphane Hessel and Elias Sanbar, *Le Rescapé et l'exilé* (Paris: Don Quichotte, 2011).

2 Ran Hazévi, "Israël: 'Une villa dans la jungle,'" *Le Débat*, 2016/3 no. 190: 154–60.

3 Ron Ben-Yishaï, "Israël est une villa dans la jungle," *Tribune juive*, June 30, 2016.

4 Ehud Barak, "L'Ombre et la lumière," *Les Temps modernes*, no. 651, November–December 2008.

5 Avraham Burg, *The Holocaust Is Over, We Must Rise from Its Ashes* (New York: St. Martin's Press, 2008), 193.

6 Avraham Burg, *The Holocaust Is Over*, 55.

7 Yeshayahu Leibowitz, *Judaism, Human Values, and the Jewish State*, ed. Eliezer Goldman, trans. Yoram Navon (Cambridge: Harvard University Press, 1992), 225–6.

8 Charles Enderlin, "Israël, le coup d'État identitaire," *Le Monde diplomatique*, February 2023.

9 See Charles Enderlin, "En Israël, l'essor de l'ultranationalisme religieux," *Le Monde diplomatique*, September 2022.

10 Yoram Hazony, *The Virtue of Nationalism*, (NY: Basic Books, 2018). See Joseph Confavreux, "Qui est Yoram Hazony, l'éminence grise de Jérusalem à Washington?" *Mediapart*, May 12, 2024, and *Revue du Crieur*, no. 24, 2024.

11 Hazony, *The Virtue of Nationalism*, 186.

12 Hazony, *The Virtue of Nationalism*, 165.

13 Collectif, *Ce que la Palestine apporte au monde* (Paris: Institut du monde arabe / Seuil, coll. Araborama, 2023).

14 Mahmoud Darwish, *Almond Blossoms and Beyond*, trans. Mohammed Shaheen (Northhampton, MA: Interlink Books, 2010), 3.

15 "Gaza: Des cinéastes du monde entier demandent un cessez-le-feu immédiat," *Libération*, December 28, 2023. The original article, published in *Haaretz* on September 22, 1967, was signed by Shimon Tzabar, Haim Hanegbi, Rafi Zichroni, David Ehrenfeld, Uri Lifschitz, Arié Boher, Dan Omer, Moshé Machover, Schneour Sherman, Raif Elias, Eli Aminov and Yehuda Rozenstrauch.

16 Moshe Machover and Elizabeth Nussbaum, "Obituary: Shimon Tzabar," *The Guardian*, April 1, 2007.

7. THE CREOLE GARDENS

1 François Héran, *Immigration. Le grand déni* (Paris: Seuil, coll. La République des Idées, 2023). See also François Héran, *Avec l'immigration. Mesurer, débattre, agir* (Paris: La Découverte, 2017), and François Héran, *Le Temps des immigrés. Essai sur le destin de la population française* (Paris: Seuil, coll. La République des Idées, 2007).

2 Aline Averbouh, Frédérique Chlous, Bruno David, Évelyne Heyer, Frédéric Jiguet, Hervé Le Bras, et al., *Migrations. Manifeste du Muséum* (Paris: Éditions du Muséum national d'histoire naturelle, 2018).

3 See Stefano Mancuso and Alessandra Viola, *Brilliant Green: The Surprising History and Science of Plant Intelligence* (Washington, DC: Island Press, 2015).

4 See Pablo Servigne and Gauthier Chapelle, *L'Entraide. L'autre loi de la jungle* (Paris: Les Liens qui libèrent, 2017).

5 See Stéphanie Besson, *Trouver refuge. Histoires vécues par-delà les frontières* (Grenoble: Glénat, 2020).

6 For more on Édouard Glissant, see his site, http://www.edouardglissant.fr/, and that of the Institut du Tout-Monde, https://www.tout-monde.com/.

7   This investigation from *Correctiv* was translated into French and published by *Mediapart*: "En Allemagne, l'extrême droite planifie secrètement la 'remigration' de millions de citoyens," January 15, 2024.

8   Video posted on X account of Republicans against Trump, November 7, 2024. https://x.com/RpsAgainstTrump/status/1854726770718585189?mx=2

9   See Florian Gouthière, "Le 'Project 2025,' une feuille de route trumpiste pour dynamiter la démocratie américaine," *Libération*, July 28, 2024; and Thomas Lemahieu, "Projet Périclès: Le document qui dit tout du plan de Pierre-Édouard Stérin pour installer le RN au pouvoir," *L'Humanité*, July 19, 2024.

8. THE TRIUMPH OF DEATH

1   "Homily of Holy Father Francis," Arena sports camp, Salina Quarter, July 8, 2013, https://www.vatican.va/content/francesco/en/homilies/2013/documents/papa-francesco_20130708_omelia-lampedusa.html/.

2   "Moment of Reflection with Religious Leaders Near the Memorial Dedicated to Sailors and Migrants Lost at Sea, Intervention of His Holiness," Marseille, September 22, 2023, https://www.vatican.va/content/francesco/en/speeches/2023/september/documents/20230922-marsiglia-leaderreligiosi.html/.

3   Robert Zaretsky, "What Netanyahu Says When He Speaks French—and Why It Borders on Obscenity," *Forward*, June 4, 2024.

4   After Yasser Arafat proclaimed the independence of Palestine in Algeria on November 15, 1988, five European states (part of the Soviet bloc at the time) recognized the State of Palestine: Hungary, Poland, Bulgaria, Romania, and Czechoslovakia (which would later split into two states, Slovakia and the Czech Republic). Cyprus and Malta did the same. Sweden joined them in 2014. Ten years later, on May 28, 2024, Spain, Ireland, and Norway recognized Palestine. They were followed by Slovenia on June 4, 2024. Because Norway is not part of the European Union, that

makes twelve out of the European Union's twenty-six states that have taken this diplomatic step at the time of this writing.

5 Arthur Berdah, Claire Conruyt, Philippe Gélie, and Vincent Trémolet de Villers, "Russie, Israël, européennes, immigration: La grande explication de Nicolas Sarkozy au *Figaro*," *Le Figaro*, May 29, 2024.

6 Jules Isaac, *The Teaching of Contempt: The Christian Roots of Anti-Semitism*, trans. Helen Weaver (New York: Holt, Rinehart and Winston, 1964).

7 André Kaspi, *Jules Isaac ou la passion de la verité* (Paris: Plon, 2002), 178.

8 Jules Isaac, *Jesus and Israel*, trans. Sally Gran (New York: Holt, Rinehart, and Winston, 1971), xxiv.

9 Isaac, *Jesus and Israel*, xix.

10 Kaspi, *Jules Isaac*, 180–81.

11 Jules Isaac, *Has Anti-Semitism Roots in Christianity?*, trans. Dorothy and James Parkes (New York: National Conference of Christians and Jews, 1961), 45.

12 Isaac, *Jesus and Israel*, 10.

13 Tzach Yoked, "How European Jews Were Labeled, Centuries Before the Yellow Star," *Haaretz*, April 21, 2023.

14 See Rodrigo de Zayas, *Les Morisques et le racisme d'État* (Paris: Éditions de la Différence, 2017).

15 Olivier Le Cour Grandmaison, *"Ennemis mortels." Représentations de l'islam et politiques musulmanes en France à l'époque coloniale* (Paris: La Découverte, 2019).

16 Ernest Renan, "Islam and Science," a lecture presented at the Sorbonne on March 29, 1883. English translation by Sally P. Ragep, McGill University, 2011, with the assistance of Prof. Faith Wallis.

17 Ernest Renan, "De la part des peuples sémitiques dans l'histoire de la civilization." In *Oeuvres complètes*, vol. 2 (Paris: Calmann-Lévy, 1948), pp. 317–35. English translation from John Tolan, Henry Laurens, and Gilles Veinstein, *Europe and the Islamic*

World: A History (Princeton and Oxford: Princeton University Press, 2012), 314.

18 Toby Greene, "The Term 'Judeo-Christian' Has Been Misused for Political Ends—a New 'Abrahamic' Identity Offers an Alternative," *The Conversation*, December 24, 2020.

19 Jules Isaac, *The Teaching of Contempt: Christian Roots of Anti-Semitism*, trans. Helen Weaver (New York: Holt, Rinehart, 1964), 20.

20 Kaspi, *Jules Isaac*, 244.

9. HUMANITY AND THE EARTH

1 Jean Guiart, *La Terre est le sang des morts. La confrontation entre Blancs et Noirs dans le Pacifique sud français*, (Paris: Éditions Anthropos, 1983).

2 Pierre Kropotkine, *Mutual Aid: A Factor of Evolution* (New York: McClure Phillips, 1903).

3 Élisée Reclus, "De l'action humaine sur la géographie physique," *Revue des deux mondes*, XXIVe année, tome cinquante-quatrième, 15 décembre 1864, pp. 762–71.

4 Élisée Reclus, *La Terre détruite par l'homme* (Paris: Espaces & Signes, 2023).

5 Élisée Reclus, *L'Homme et la Terre. Histoire contemporaine*, 6 vol. (Paris: Fayard, 1990).

6 Élisée Reclus, *L'Homme et la Terre*, 533.

7 Élisée Reclus, *L'Homme et la Terre*, 540–41.

8 Alexandre Dumas, *My Memoirs*, trans. E. M. Waller (NY: Macmillan, 1907), 167–68.

9 Alexandre Dumas, *Le Mois* (tomes 1 à 2, mars 1848–novembre 1849) 1849, p. 6.

10 Albert Camus, "Albert Camus's Speech at the Nobel Banquet at the City Hall in Stockholm, December 10, 1957," The Nobel Foundation, https://www.nobelprize.org/prizes/literature/1957/camus/speech/.